The Million-Dollar Nightmare

Suddenly, without warning, the big black stallion whinnied and reared on its hind legs. Frank froze and then backpedaled as fast as he could.

"Run for the fence!" Frank shouted.

Now the horse was charging after them. Joe ran toward his brother, stumbling in the grass. Hooves thundered behind them, forcing them to keep running around the perimeter of the small fenced paddock.

Finally Frank saw his chance. He ducked under the fence railing to safety, rolling in the grass to make sure he was clear of the wild stallion. But when he stood up and turned around, his heart nearly stopped.

Joe had tripped and fallen—and the stallion was rearing above Joe's head, ready to trample him to death!

The Hardy Boys Mystery Stories

Available from MINSTREL Books

103

The

HARDY BOYS®

THE MILLION-DOLLAR NIGHTMARE

FRANKLIN W. DIXON

A MINSTREL® BOOK

PUBLISHED BY POCKET BOOKS

New York   London   Toronto   Sydney   Tokyo   Singapore

A MINSTREL PAPERBACK *ORIGINAL*

A Minstrel Book published by
POCKET BOOKS, a division of Simon & Schuster Inc.
1230 Avenue of the Americas, New York, NY 10020

Copyright © 1990 by Simon & Schuster Inc.
Cover artwork copyright © 1990 by Paul Bachem
Produced by Mega-Books of New York, Inc.

ISBN: 0-671-69272-0

First Minstrel Books printing August 1990

10 9 8 7 6 5 4 3 2 1

Contents

1 Mysterious Encounter

"I can't believe I'm doing this," Joe Hardy muttered. He stopped in the middle of the crowded city block and pulled a hooded sweatshirt over his head. His thick blond hair poked through first, followed by his sparkling blue eyes and then his broad smile. Even in a bulky sweatshirt, Joe's six-foot frame still looked compact and muscular. "I mean, it's July and I'm wearing a sweatshirt."

Frank Hardy, bundled in a thick fisherman's sweater, stood next to his brother. Eighteen and a year older than Joe, Frank was taller, thinner, and quieter, too. The cool wet breeze blew his straight dark hair into his face. "Hey—welcome to San

1

Francisco, Joe," Frank said with a laugh. "It'll warm up when the fog burns off . . . around September."

The two brothers smiled at each other and then looked around. They were spending a week of their summer vacation on the other side of the country from their hometown of Bayport, three thousand miles away. Leaving home also meant that they'd left behind their reputation as the two hottest teenage detectives on the East Coast.

"So what do we do first?" Joe said. "Go see the buffalo in Golden Gate Park? Ride a cable car? Walk across the Golden Gate Bridge?"

"Sounds good for starters," Frank joked. "Then in the afternoon we can *really* get into some sightseeing."

"Hey, I'm not kidding," Joe said. "I mean, we have only two days here, before we have to drive down to Los Angeles to meet Dad. We've got to pack as much stuff into these two days as possible. I say we do the cable cars and Fisherman's Wharf this morning, the ocean, the beach, and Golden Gate Park in the afternoon, and then take a ferryboat ride to Sausalito tonight. Are you up for it? Frank? Hello, Frank? Hey—what are you staring at?"

But Frank wasn't listening to his brother. Instead he was staring a few feet ahead at a huge man in a black suit who was coming straight toward them.

2

Frank guessed that the man weighed at least two hundred and fifty pounds.

"Look," Frank said under his breath. "Look who it is."

"Who?"

"The guy with the walking stick."

The large man was moving straight forward at a good pace as if he expected everyone and everything in his path to move out of the way. But Frank was too surprised to move. He stood frozen in the middle of the sidewalk, still staring, with his mouth hanging open.

"Pardon me," the large man said, motioning with his shiny black walking stick.

Frank stepped aside to let the man pass and then elbowed his brother. "Did you see who that was?"

"No. Who?"

"Come on," Frank replied.

It took Joe less than half a second to realize that his brother was following the stranger down the street, and less than another half second to catch up. "Why are we following him?" Joe asked.

"Did you see that walking stick? It had a gold horse-head handle. That's got to be Julian Ardyce!" Frank said softly.

"What are you talking about?" Joe didn't even try to hide his frustration.

"Oh, yeah, I forgot. You didn't see the television show the other night, did you? 'America's Most Mysterious Unsolved Crimes.'"

3

Joe shook his head. It was his favorite TV show, but he had missed the most recent episode while packing for the flight to San Francisco. "He was on the show?" Joe asked, trying to get a better look at the man they were following. "What did he do?"

"Three years ago," Frank said, "a million-dollar racehorse named Nightmare disappeared. It was owned by some people named Roger and Barbara Glass and their daughter, Nina. They've got a horse farm somewhere around San Francisco." As Frank talked, he and Joe kept following the large man in the black suit with the horse-head walking stick.

Suddenly the man stopped to listen to a saxophone player on a busy street corner. The Hardys quickly turned and looked in a store window so they wouldn't be noticed.

"He's giving the musician a five-dollar bill and walking again," Joe said, watching the man's reflection in the window. "Okay. Let's go."

"So anyway," Frank continued, picking up his story, "on the show they interviewed the suspects. There was a jockey named Billy Morales, a groom named Danny Chaps, and Nightmare's trainer, Buzz McCord, who worked for the Glasses. Any or all of them might have been in on it, but Julian Ardyce was suspect number one."

"How come?"

"Because he had the most to gain," Frank explained. "He was a rival horse owner, and when Nightmare disappeared, his horse won the race."

"I get it," Joe said, nodding quickly.

"But the police could never prove that Ardyce stole the horse, so they had to let him go. And right after that, he disappeared! According to the TV show, no one has seen him since. They showed a photograph of him on TV and said he was famous for carrying a walking stick with a solid gold horse-head handle."

"Wow! If we could solve this mystery, they'd put us on the TV show."

"I know," Frank said wistfully. "But we have to be in L.A. in two days to meet Dad."

"No problem," Joe said. "We've got half the case solved right now. Julian Ardyce is in our sights, right? Maybe if we just follow him around for a few hours, he'll lead us straight to that missing horse!"

"Sounds good to me," Frank said, shaking his head. Both he and his brother knew that few mysteries were that easy to solve.

A moment later Julian Ardyce turned into the entrance of a large San Francisco bank. Frank followed right behind him, pushing through the tall revolving doors and into the glass-and-marble lobby. He and Joe got in line behind Ardyce after letting an older woman go in front of them. The waiting line was the best place to watch from, Frank decided. That way, even when Ardyce reached the teller, Frank would be in position to see and hear every detail.

Pretty soon Ardyce was standing only a few feet in front of Frank. He laid his walking stick across the smooth marble counter and said good morning to the teller. Then he took a thick stack of fifty-dollar bills and a single deposit slip from the inside pocket of his jacket. The teller took the money, counted it twice, and gave him a receipt. Then Ardyce picked up his walking stick and left the bank.

The Hardys followed quickly behind him. But just as they got to the door, the bank guard stepped in front of them. "Hey, fellas," he said, blocking their path. "It's free umbrella day." He handed each of them an umbrella with the name of the bank on the stalk.

"Uh, no thanks," Frank said as the brothers spun through the heavy revolving door, looking up and down the street for Julian Ardyce. But the delay had slowed them down.

"He got away," Joe muttered.

Frank scanned the street, sidewalk, store entrances, and passing cars.

"No, he didn't," Frank said. "He's going into that restaurant across the street. Let's go!"

They darted across the street and into the Soup Bowl, a small, sunny restaurant crowded with hanging plants and hungry customers. Julian Ardyce had already been seated at the last available table. Frank and Joe had to wait in line. By the time they got a table, Ardyce was leaning back in his seat,

6

breaking crackers into a bowl of chili. He was sitting near a back exit at a table with a red-haired man. The other man was middle-aged, his face lined and dry from the sun. He leaned forward, his elbows on the table, talking quickly to Ardyce.

Frank watched closely but couldn't hear a word of the conversation from where he was.

"They look like old friends," Joe said quietly to Frank. "And the red-haired guy looks as if he's spent time on a ranch or farm. Do you recognize him?"

"No." Frank shook his head. "He wasn't on the TV show."

"I wonder what brought Julian Ardyce out of hiding after three years?" Joe whispered.

"What? I can barely hear you," Frank said, leaning toward his brother.

The restaurant had been noisy with the sounds of people talking, silverware clinking, and music playing on the stereo system. But suddenly Frank realized that another sound was filling the space. It was a low, ominous rumble that sounded like a freight train roaring by at full speed. And it came from right under Frank's chair.

Almost immediately the floor began to shake—a little at first, then more, until Frank felt the floor actually roll under his feet like a roller coaster. Instinctively he grabbed the edge of the table and held on, but the dishes rattled and glasses crashed to the floor.

7

"Get down! Get under the tables!" several people shouted.

A hard pounding lump formed in Frank's chest as he realized all at once what was happening. It was an earthquake! Quickly, almost automatically, people jumped out of their seats, crawled under the tables, and crouched on the floor on their hands and knees.

Frank and Joe quickly did the same. The table shook above them, and some soup spilled, dripping over the edge onto the floor.

And then, in the next moment, the earthquake stopped—not quickly, but gradually. The noise slowly faded away, and the floor stopped rolling. The quake had lasted only about fifteen seconds. But the patrons in the restaurant didn't move until they were sure it was over.

Frank looked at his younger brother, crouching face-to-face with him under the table. They were both trembling and breathing hard. "So that's an earthquake," Frank said.

"Awesome ride," Joe said, getting to his feet a little shakily.

"A three-pointer," said a gray-haired woman at the table next to them.

"Felt like a three-point-five quake to me," said her gray-haired companion, who was wearing a flowered hat.

Frank and Joe had read enough about earth-

8

quakes to know that the women were estimating the earthquake's rating on the Richter scale.

"I've lived here all my life," said the first elderly woman. "I can read a quake better than I can read the newspaper. That one wasn't bad, believe me."

Frank looked around, amazed. Once again people in the restaurant were sitting at their tables, talking to their friends, eating their lunch, while the restaurant help cleaned up the few dishes that had broken. Everyone was so calm about it—as though it happened every day.

"Frank! Look!" Joe said, pointing at an empty table behind them.

Frank slapped the side of his leg in disappointment. Somehow, during or after the earthquake, the two men who had been sitting there had slipped away. Julian Ardyce was gone!

2 A Horse Tale

Frank and Joe hurried out of the restaurant and looked up and down the street. There was no sign of Julian Ardyce, and to Joe's surprise there wasn't much commotion outside, either. People were walking, talking, and laughing, almost as if the earthquake hadn't happened at all.

"I guess people around here are used to it," Joe said with a shrug.

"We're not used to it. We just don't sweat the small stuff," said a woman passing by, who had overheard his comment.

Joe laughed. "Well, so what do we do about Ardyce?"

"He shouldn't be too hard to find," Frank said. "Especially since he must live around here."

"How do we know that?"

"Think about it. Ardyce deposited a lot of money in that bank, and he didn't use one of the bank's deposit slips. He used his own."

"Right. He must have an account there," Joe said. "So he probably lives somewhere in the Bay Area."

"We could check the phone books, but I'll bet he's not listed," Frank said. "He might even be using an alias. I think our best move is to try to find the Glass family."

Within an hour, Frank and Joe had found an address and phone number for Roger and Barbara Glass and their horse ranch, Stallion Canyon. There were two numbers, in fact, but when Frank dialed the number for the Glasses' residence, the phone just rang and rang with no answer. When he dialed the number for the ranch, Frank got an answering machine. He hung up the pay phone and looked at Joe.

"Looks like you get to see twenty-seven tourist attractions in twelve hours, after all," Frank said with a laugh.

"Great!" Joe said, his stomach growling audibly. "Let's catch a cable car to Fisherman's Wharf and have lunch. We'll call these numbers every half hour, and if they don't answer by the end of the day, we'll check out the place tomorrow in person."

Early the next morning Frank and Joe called the garage in their hotel and asked for their car to be sent to the front entrance. It was a small white Chevy—a car their father had rented for them at the airport before he'd flown to Los Angeles.

"How long do you think it'll take us to get to Stallion Canyon?" Joe asked as his brother climbed behind the wheel.

"About an hour—maybe more," Frank said. "I hope someone is home when we get there. It's too early to call the Glasses right now."

Joe ate a breakfast of doughnuts and milk as Frank drove across the Golden Gate Bridge. Then they headed north for more than an hour to the rolling hills of Sonoma County. The hills were golden in summer, browned out from the heat and the usual lack of rain. Frank couldn't get used to the idea that everything in California was brown in the summer, green in the winter. The farther north they drove, the warmer it got.

"You know, I think we're really on to something with this case," Joe said as Frank drove.

"Why? We've hardly gotten started."

"I know," Joe said. "But think about it. We've seen Julian Ardyce—the prime suspect in the disappearance of that horse. We know that Ardyce vanished afterward. And we saw him deposit a lot of cash in the bank. Where do you guess he got all that money?"

"Tell me, little brother, because I know you're dying to."

12

"I think he has Nightmare," Joe said. "He's either racing him secretly somewhere, and that money was his winnings from a private bet, or . . . maybe he sold Nightmare!"

"They're both good theories," Frank admitted. "I hope the first one is right. If that horse has been sold, it could be halfway around the world by now. We'll ask the Glasses what they think when we get to Stallion Canyon."

Joe checked the map. "Turn here. We're almost there."

Frank followed his brother's directions and found a long winding dirt road that led to Stallion Canyon. It was a small horse ranch tucked in a valley and surrounded by tall hills covered with golden brown grass. All around the property was a brown split-rail fence, but the gate was open. Frank drove in and stopped the car when they came to a house, the first of four gray wooden buildings.

The Hardys stepped out of their car into the hot sun.

"Now, this is more like summer," Joe said, peeling off his sweatshirt and tucking in his T-shirt.

Before they even approached the house, the front door opened and a girl came out. She was about the Hardys' age or a little younger and was pretty, with curly dark hair and large green eyes. Her thin, graceful arms and legs looked more like a ballet dancer's than a ranch hand's. She was wearing

13

jeans, riding boots, and a pale peach-colored T-shirt with a small silver and turquoise beaded necklace. In her pierced ears she wore small silver earrings. Frank immediately recognized her from the television program. She was Nina Glass.

She looked at them quizzically. "May I help you?"

"We're looking for Roger and Barbara Glass," Joe said. "We have some information about Nightmare."

A look of surprise flashed across Nina's face, making her pale skin turn even paler. She held her breath, as if she could barely wait for Frank to say something more.

"I'm Frank Hardy," Frank said, extending his hand to shake. "And this is my brother, Joe. You must be Nina Glass. Are your parents around?"

"Nightmare was *my* horse," Nina said. She seemed about to burst with hope and curiosity. "If you know something about him, tell *me.*"

But before the Hardys could answer, a tall, thin man with gold-wire glasses and hair as dark as Nina's came out the front door and stood behind her.

"Neen, you didn't tell me you had company," the man said with a big smile.

Nina quickly introduced Frank and Joe to her father, and the Hardys explained why they were there.

14

"We saw Julian Ardyce in San Francisco yesterday. I think he's living somewhere in the Bay Area. We're detectives, and we thought maybe we could help find Nightmare," Frank said.

Roger Glass's eyes lit up, and Frank could see that his attention was undivided. Roger gave Nina a quick glance.

"Come inside," he said to the Hardys, making a large, welcoming gesture with one arm.

As they sat down on a long, low couch in the living room, Roger Glass sent his daughter to the kitchen to get a pitcher of iced tea for their guests. The minute she left the room, he turned to the Hardys and lowered his voice.

"Now, listen," Roger said to them. "I don't know if you guys are for real or not. I got about ten calls right after that TV program aired, all of them offering to help find Nightmare. But here's what you've got to understand. There's nothing I'd like more in this world than to have that horse back. But I don't want Nina to get hurt. It broke her heart when Nightmare was stolen. Whatever happens, I don't want you to get her all worked up about this again, only to find out that the horse is long gone."

"Don't treat me like a baby, Dad."

Nina stood in the living room archway with her hands on her hips.

"Nina, where's the iced tea?" her father asked, flushing slightly.

15

"It's too early for snacks," Nina said. "And besides, Frank and Joe aren't thirsty. I can tell. Now, let's talk about my horse."

Joe laughed and flashed Nina his famous smile—the one he often used to charm information out of unsuspecting suspects. Only this time the smile was for real. Nina smiled back at Joe and curled up in an overstuffed chair with her legs tucked under her.

"We're telling the truth, Mr. Glass," Frank began. "Yesterday we saw a man who fit exactly Julian Ardyce's description, and I think there's a good chance we can at least find out what happened to Nightmare—even if we don't get the horse back. What we'd like first is for you to tell us what happened the day Nightmare was stolen. Everything you can remember, from beginning to end."

Roger Glass was quiet for a moment. Then he nodded at his daughter, and she began telling the story earnestly, as if it had happened just the week before.

"It was at the California Classic—the biggest race in this state," she began. "We drove down to the track a few days before the race, and we took Nightmare with us. He was boarded in a stable at the track, just like the other horses that were going to race."

"Who was watching him?" interrupted Joe.

"We took a groom, Danny Chaps, with us. And of course Buzz McCord, Nightmare's trainer, came along. Each day before the race, Buzz would work

16

him out a little, to keep him fit. Anyway, everything went fine until the day of the race."

"What happened?" Frank asked.

"I don't know," Nina said. "But I sensed that something was wrong the minute I saw Nightmare that morning. I got up early and went to the stable to see him. He was jittery—as though he knew something was going to happen. I thought maybe he was sick or maybe someone had been in his stall, messing around with him. But the vet at the track said he checked out fine, so I didn't worry too much. Then another weird thing happened. Billy Morales, the jockey who was supposed to ride Nightmare, showed up at the track four hours early. He said he wanted to take a look at Nightmare before the race."

"That doesn't sound so strange to me," Joe said. "If I were a jockey riding in a big race, I'd want to take the horse for a test drive first, too."

Nina laughed and Joe looked embarrassed.

"Maybe you would," said Roger Glass, "but most jockeys don't do that. In fact, usually they don't see the horse they're going to ride until right before a race."

"Well, anyway," Nina went on, "at about noon Dad and I got dressed for the race and went to the special section of the spectators' box that's reserved for owners. Buzz McCord met us there. We had lunch, and everything seemed to be okay. But about thirty minutes before post time, Danny Chaps sent

17

a note up to our box saying that Billy Morales had left the track and still hadn't come back. Before we could do anything, Danny came running in himself, shouting that Nightmare was gone!

"We ran like crazy to the stable," Nina continued, "and found a horse in Nightmare's box. But it wasn't Nightmare. It was a horse that looked like Nightmare."

"How did you know it wasn't Nightmare?" Joe asked.

"The horse in Nightmare's stall had a white stocking," said Mr. Glass.

He took a silver-framed photo of Nightmare from the mantel and handed it to Joe and Frank. He pointed out that the sleek, beautiful black horse had no white markings, or stockings, on its legs.

"The police figured out how it happened later," Nina explained. "Someone substituted Julian Ardyce's horse, Spats, for Nightmare. They must have painted a white stocking on Nightmare so he'd look like Spats. Then they put Nightmare in a trailer and drove him away."

"But how could they just drive the horse away?" Joe asked. "Aren't there guards at a racetrack?"

Mr. Glass nodded. "There are. And they check the horse's release papers before letting any trailer leave. The way we figure it, whoever stole Nightmare had release papers for Spats. Later, when the police questioned him, the guard said he checked through a black horse with a white stocking on its

18

left front leg. It matched the release paper, so he let the trailer go."

"Yeah—and he didn't even bother to check the tattoo," Nina said angrily.

"What tattoo?" Frank asked.

"Every thoroughbred horse that's been raced has a number tattooed inside its lip," Nina answered. "The guards are *supposed* to check it before they let any horse leave the grounds. But they usually don't."

Suddenly there was a loud pounding on the ranch house door.

Roger Glass looked around in annoyance. "What now?" he said to Nina.

"Come on in!" she called, slowly climbing out of her comfortable chair to answer the door.

But before she was up, a ranch hand burst into the living room, out of breath from running.

"It's your horse!" he called to Nina. "It's Blue Rider! He's gone!"

19

3 A Short Ride

A look of panic crossed Nina's pretty face, and her forehead wrinkled deeply. "No! Not again!" she cried.

With a pleading glance toward Frank, she ran from the room and out of the house, letting the screen door bang behind her.

Frank and Joe jumped up and followed at top speed, running all the way down the winding dirt road to the barn.

How could this be? Frank wondered as they ran. How could another of Nina Glass's horses have been stolen—right out from under her nose?

When he got to the barn, Frank slowed his pace so he wouldn't frighten the horses. With his brother close behind, he quietly crept past the rows of straw-filled boxes and narrow stalls that filled the barn. Curious stallions stuck their heads over the wooden half-doors, snorting and sniffing nervously. At the end of the row he found Nina. But she was smiling!

"Jerry, you forgot to lock Blue Rider's door, didn't you?" she said, scolding a stable boy who was standing nearby. Nina inspected the lock. "You know Blue Rider can open the door latch with his nose. I'll bet I know where he is."

With a smile in the Hardys' direction, Nina ran out to a field, calling back, "I'll meet you at the house in a few minutes!"

Twenty minutes later she returned, reporting that Blue Rider had merely escaped to his favorite field. Then she and the Hardys sat in the Glasses' living room, drinking iced tea and eating lunch. This time Roger had prepared the food and drinks himself.

They all sat around a low square coffee table, eating tuna fish sandwiches and fresh fruit.

"So where were we when my daughter's second horse disappeared?" Roger asked with a smile.

"You were telling us how Nightmare was stolen," Frank answered. "But what about suspects?"

"I thought the TV show said Julian Ardyce was the prime suspect," Joe said.

"That's what I thought at the time—and it's what the police thought, too," said Roger Glass dryly. "For a whole lot of reasons. Number one, I guess, is that Julian has the kind of personality that

21

makes you think he'd do anything to win. He's a power player—if you know what I mean."

"And his horse won the California Classic after Nightmare disappeared?" Frank asked.

Roger nodded. "That horse could never have won if Nightmare had been running. Also someone claimed to have seen Julian near Nightmare's stall before the race."

Joe looked puzzled.

"Owners don't go near their own horses before a race," Nina explained. "Handling the horse is the trainer's job, and the groom's."

"So why couldn't the police nail Ardyce?" Joe asked as he picked up a second tuna sandwich.

"There just wasn't any hard evidence," Roger Glass said. "Sure, Spats, the horse that was in Nightmare's stall, was Julian's horse. But as Julian argued to the police, anyone could have switched the horses. And to prove that he didn't do it, he still had Spats's release papers."

"So the thief must have used forged release papers," Frank chimed in. "But that doesn't rule Ardyce out. He could have forged the papers, too."

"True," Roger agreed. "But Julian also pointed out that all of his horse trailers were still on the grounds of the racetrack. And besides, there were other suspects."

"Who?" asked Frank.

"They're all right here." Roger Glass put down

22

his drink and walked over to a large oak desk. He took another framed photo out of the bottom drawer. In the photo was a short man in racing silks, sitting on a horse with a garland of roses around its neck. "That's the jockey, Billy Morales," said Roger Glass.

Frank looked at the picture closely. Standing next to the horse were Mr. and Mrs. Glass and Nina. On the opposite side of the horse was a tall, wiry young man wearing a turned-around baseball cap. Roger explained that he was Danny Chaps, the groom. The last one in the picture was a big man wearing a ten-gallon hat pulled low so that it almost touched his mirrored sunglasses.

"Who's this?" Frank asked, pointing.

"That's Buzz McCord, the trainer," Roger replied.

"Okay," Frank said, thinking hard and staring at the photo. "You said Buzz McCord was with you in your box when Nightmare was stolen. And Billy Morales came to see Nightmare in the morning, but then he left and never came back. Right?"

"Right," Nina said, wiping crumbs from her mouth with her napkin. "Later he told the police that he left because he wasn't feeling well. But everyone at the stable said that Billy seemed nervous and upset about something that day."

"Exactly what time was Nightmare stolen?"

"It was between two o'clock and two forty-five,"

Nina answered. "We know because Danny Chaps and the vet swore that Nightmare was still in his stall at two. Danny was grooming him."

"Does Danny have an alibi?" Frank asked.

"He said he was buying a can of soda when Nightmare was stolen," Nina said. "And lots of people in the stable said they saw him buying it."

"Convenient disappearance. That's what an accomplice does best," Frank murmured.

"Are Buzz and Danny here?" Joe asked. "We'd like to talk to them."

Mr. Glass shook his head. "Buzz quit a few months after Nightmare was stolen. He started his own brood-mare farm a few miles north of here. He's doing really well."

"A brood-mare farm?" Joe asked.

"A breeding ranch for thoroughbreds," Roger explained.

"What happened to Danny Chaps?" Joe asked.

"Dad fired him after we found out that he used to work for Ardyce," Nina answered. "We started finding out that we couldn't really trust Danny."

The Hardys looked at each other. Frank could see Joe running through the possible suspects in his head: Julian Ardyce, Danny Chaps, Billy Morales —and who else? There might have been someone else hanging around the stable that day, someone who had the motive, the means, and the opportunity to steal Nightmare. Frank was beginning to see why this case had remained unsolved for so long.

"Well?" Nina said, breaking the silence. "Do you think there's any chance you could really find Nightmare?"

"We're going to try," Frank said. Then he turned to Joe. "Why don't we go to Buzz McCord's ranch? He might be able to tell us something—like where Julian Ardyce lives."

Frank and Joe carried their empty plates to the kitchen and thanked Roger Glass for the lunch.

"One last question," Joe said. "Why steal Nightmare at all? I mean, nobody can ever race him again in public, because he'd be recognized for sure."

"It's possible that someone is racing him privately," Roger Glass said. "In fact, people do it all the time in Mexico. There's heavy betting on those races, too. But Nightmare doesn't have to run another step to be worth millions in stud fees."

"People would pay hundreds of thousands for a chance to mate their brood mares with him," said Nina.

Mr. Glass looked sadly at Nightmare's photo in the silver frame. "For a small breeding ranch like ours, a horse like Nightmare comes along once in a lifetime. We bred him here, and he was perfect. We'll probably never have another horse like that."

Nina got up from her seat. "I'll show Frank and Joe where Buzz's ranch is," she told her father. She turned to the Hardys. "It's only a few miles from Stallion Canyon, but the road twists and turns up a mountain, so it'll take a while to get there. I can fill you in on some more details on the way."

Twenty minutes later they arrived at a beautiful piece of property high on a cliff overlooking the Pacific Ocean. Joe noticed right away that the place was twice the size of Roger Glass's ranch. There were more barns and outbuildings, all painted white, and there were more horses in evidence, too. As they entered the ranch through a very well maintained high-security gate, Joe saw that Buzz had several exercise corrals and each was crowded with beautiful mares and their foals.

"I thought McCord used to work for you," Joe said. "Why does he have a bigger ranch?"

"Trainers make big money, especially if they work with a lot of great horses," Nina said.

"You mean like Nightmare?" Frank said.

Nina nodded. "And Nightmare wasn't the only champion Buzz trained," she added.

"Try to get Buzz to show us around the ranch," Joe said as his eyes scanned the property. "Maybe we'll pick up some clues."

"Okay," Nina said. "I can do that. Hey! There he is!" She pointed ahead, rolled down the window, and called, "Buzz!"

Joe pulled up to a gravel parking area and saw a man in blue jeans, snakeskin cowboy boots, and a red-checked shirt. He turned around when he heard his name called. He stuffed his hands in his back pockets and walked slowly toward the car.

Buzz McCord was in his forties with a muscular chest that bulged under his shirt. The brim of his white cowboy hat was tipped low, almost touching the top of his mirrored sunglasses.

"Howdy, Nina," Buzz McCord said.

Nina started to open the back door and get out, but Buzz leaned into the open back window on her side.

"Haven't seen you in months. How are your mom and dad?"

"They're doing okay, Buzz," Nina said. "I'd like you to meet Frank and Joe Hardy. They're detectives, and we're going to find Nightmare."

Out of the corner of his eye, Frank Hardy saw his brother squirm. Nina was telling Buzz too much—and expecting too much. What if they couldn't deliver?

"I'll bet you fellas saw that TV show," Buzz said, poking his head in Frank's window now. A big grin spread across McCord's face. "Is that it? You boys hoping to solve a big mystery and get yourselves on television?"

McCord's grin said he doubted they could find the horse, and his tone was mocking, too.

"We saw Julian Ardyce in San Francisco yesterday," Joe said.

Buzz let that sink in for a minute. "Ardyce? In San Francisco?" The smile faded quickly. "Are you sure?"

"No mistake," Joe said confidently.

"Okay," Buzz said. "Why don't you get out of the car and we'll talk."

I would have gotten out sooner, Frank thought to himself, if you hadn't been blocking my way. Frank swung open his door, and McCord stepped back.

"We'd like to hear your version of what happened the day Nightmare was stolen," Frank said.

"I don't have much of a story, and I told it to the police a couple of dozen times," Buzz said. He sighed and told it again. "I spent the morning with Nightmare, warming him up, checking him out, me and Danny Chaps. The horse was fine. He was ready to run. So at noon I got cleaned up and went to the spectators' box to have lunch with Nina and her dad. Next thing I knew, Danny came running up and told us Nightmare was gone."

"And my dad and I told you everything that happened after that," Nina said, cutting off Buzz's story.

Frank smiled but shook his head slightly at Nina. Didn't she understand? It didn't matter what her father had said. He and Joe needed to hear the whole story from Buzz McCord. If it was even a little bit different, they would have something to investigate.

"What about Julian Ardyce?" Frank asked. "Did you see him around the stables that day?"

"I wish I had. Wish I could have nailed this on Ardyce a long time ago," Buzz said.

"Do you think he stole Nightmare?" Joe asked.

28

"Truth is, maybe it was Ardyce. But maybe it was another owner, maybe even some outsiders. The way people come and go in the stables on race day, it wouldn't surprise me to find out that the queen of England walked in there and stole that horse."

"We're going to narrow it down," Joe said sarcastically, "and just question the people who *were* there."

"Well, don't get too discouraged," said Buzz.

"Buzz, can we take a ride?" Nina asked, shooting a glance at the Hardys. "I haven't ridden Will-o'-the-Wisp in a long time. And I'll bet Frank and Joe would love to see what a real brood-mare farm looks like. They're not from around here. They're easterners."

"No kidding," Buzz said, his mirrored sunglasses masking his expression.

Cool move, Nina, Frank thought to himself. This was their chance to look around Buzz's ranch.

"I don't know, Nina," Buzz said, hesitating. "These guys look more like freeway jockeys than riders."

"We've ridden before," Frank said.

"Please, Buzz," said Nina, tossing her curly black hair and giving him a huge smile.

"Well, okay. I'll saddle up some horses. Meet me at the end of that barn." He gestured toward one of the white buildings.

Buzz walked away from the Hardys, leaving Frank, Joe, and Nina standing in the parking lot.

"It's funny," Joe said when Buzz was gone. "I don't see any guards, but it feels like there's real tight security here. That's strange for a farm."

"There's a reason for that," Nina said. "These horses are valuable—and they get stolen. Remember?"

Joe felt his face flush.

"Come on," Nina said, heading toward the barn. "I think Buzz is ready for us."

Frank looked toward the barn and saw Buzz coming out, riding a spirited dappled horse. He was leading a bay horse by its reins. Behind him, a young stable hand with dirty blond hair and dusty pants was leading two other horses out of the barn. One horse was chestnut brown and one pure black.

"Well, mount up, cowboys!" Buzz called with a laugh.

Nina quickly climbed into the saddle of the bay horse. She petted him and called him Will-o'-the-Wisp. Then Joe mounted the chestnut horse.

That left the tall black horse for Frank. Weird, Frank thought. Here I am riding one black stallion and looking for another. As the stable hand adjusted the stirrups, Frank heard the guy whisper something, something he couldn't understand.

"What?" Frank asked.

The young stable hand said it again, slower but not louder. "You're looking for Julian Ardyce?"

Frank pretended to help adjust the saddle straps.

30

"There's a rumor that Ardyce owns Wind Ridge Farm," the guy whispered.

Amazing, Frank thought. How did he know I was looking for Ardyce? He gave the stable hand a questioning stare.

"Let's ride," Buzz called from a few feet away.

Questions raced through Frank's mind as he swung into the saddle. Where was Wind Ridge Farm? And why was this guy telling him about it?

But as soon as Frank mounted, the questions flew out of his head—because all of a sudden, without warning, the black stallion took off. He bolted past the others and ran wildly down the road. Frank's body jerked backward, and he almost fell off. His hands gripped the horse's mane, clinging to it desperately.

From behind him, Frank could hear someone shouting at him, but he didn't know what they were saying because the world was flying by in a blur.

And then, just as suddenly as he'd taken off, the horse stopped and bucked, sending Frank flying through the air, as if he had been launched from the saddle!

4 Cold Welcome

Joe's heart jumped into his throat as he watched his brother hit the ground with a thud. Frank lay motionless, unconscious, his face pressed to the ground, his arms and legs sprawled crookedly. For just an instant, Joe was motionless, too, frozen with fear. Was his brother unconscious—or was he dead?

Then Joe bolted into action, jumping from the chestnut and running to his brother's side. "Frank!" he cried, dropping to his knees.

"Is he okay?" asked Nina, after dismounting and rushing up to stand behind Joe.

"I don't know." Joe practically whispered the words. He reached out to turn Frank over.

"Whoa! Better handle him easy." Buzz McCord's voice was strong and commanding. "He may have broken something."

Yeah, thanks to your horse, Joe thought.

Buzz had grabbed the reins of the black horse that had thrown Frank, and he was petting his nose, trying to calm him down. Then he held out the reins for Nina to hold. He knelt down with Joe. "Let's take it slow," Buzz said.

Cautiously Joe and Buzz turned Frank over. His face was smudged with dirt. His forehead was scraped and bleeding. Joe quickly felt for a pulse in Frank's neck.

"Is he okay?" Nina asked again, only this time her voice cracked.

"He's breathing," Joe said, finally letting out a long breath of his own.

"Looks like he just got banged up," Buzz said. "He'll probably come around in a minute."

Just then Frank opened his eyes. At first he looked as if he didn't recognize Joe. Then he smiled a little. "Well," Frank said weakly, "I know I'm not in heaven, because you're still just as goofy-looking as you were before."

Joe laughed. "Too bad a bump on the head didn't improve your jokes any."

With Buzz and Joe's help, Frank sat up. But Joe could tell Frank still felt dizzy and light-headed.

"What happened?" Frank asked groggily.

"You lost control of your horse—that's what happened," Buzz said.

"That horse was too wild for anyone to control," Frank said, beginning to remember.

Buzz shook his head. "You've got Blackbeard all wrong. He loves to be ridden—by riders who know what they're doing. I thought you said you knew how to ride."

I do know how to ride, Frank thought to himself. I also know that horse is wild—or else something startled him.

"I guess you want a rain check on seeing my ranch?" Buzz asked.

"Yeah, I guess so," Frank said. He stood up, unsteady on his legs at first, and then slapped the dust off his clothes.

"Well, we're not going anywhere," Buzz said. "Come back anytime, and I'll try to keep you in one piece so you can find Nina's horse."

He reached out to shake Frank's hand. It was a firm handshake—almost too firm, Frank thought, as if Buzz wanted him to know how strong he was.

The last thing Buzz said, before they drove away from his farm, was "Good luck, boys. And remember: if I can do anything to help you find Nightmare, call me." He gave Nina a big smile. "Don't worry, Nina," he added. "These boys inspire my confidence."

When they were off Buzz's property, Frank asked Nina about Wind Ridge Farm.

34

"It's a horse farm not too far from here," she answered. "Bill Barnell owns it. Why?"

"Because maybe Julian Ardyce owns it," Frank said.

"Where'd you hear that?" Joe asked. "Straight from the horse's mouth?"

"The stable hand," Frank said. "He was going to tell me more, but something made my horse bolt."

Joe was quick to pick up on his brother's suspicions. "You think that guy scared the horse?"

"He did," Frank said, "or Buzz did."

"Buzz? No way!" Nina said. "He's known my parents for years. They started Stallion Canyon together. He's not a suspect."

"*Everyone* is a suspect," Joe corrected. Then he turned back to his brother. "So what about Wind Ridge Farm? Think we should head over there next?"

"Maybe," Frank said. "It might be a good lead — or it might be a false one, to throw us off the track. But it's worth checking out."

"Great!" Nina said. "I'll show you where it is."

"Uh-uh." Frank shook his head. "This time we go alone."

An hour later, after dropping Nina at Stallion Canyon, the Hardys were driving north again, looking for Wind Ridge Farm. They found it about fifteen miles north of Buzz McCord's ranch, but farther inland, nestled in the hills of Sonoma County. For miles and miles they drove along beside a white three-rail fence that seemed to stretch out forever.

"Hey, it's going to take a detective just to find the barns," Joe joked. "This place is five times as big as Buzz McCord's ranch."

Finally they reached the gate. Wind Ridge Farm, Bill Barnell, Owner, a sign on the fence told them. It also said Trespassers Keep Out!

"Not too friendly," Joe said, driving the car slowly through the gate.

"Maybe they have something to hide," Frank said.

"What do we do if we see Julian Ardyce on the ranch?" Joe asked.

Frank thought about Julian Ardyce, the tall, huge man in the black suit carrying the ebony walking stick with the gold horse-head handle.

"I can think of a few questions I'd like to ask him," Frank said. "But first things first. One of us better try to get a job here, so we can start snooping around from the inside."

"I can't wait," Joe said. "I've always wanted to spend my vacation mucking out horse stalls."

Frank laughed because he knew that was Joe's way of volunteering for the job. Cleaning up after horses wouldn't be much fun, but that was probably the only kind of job Joe could get. Frank also knew that Joe loved to go under cover, and being on the

36

inside at Wind Ridge Farm might lead to some real clues that would crack the case.

Joe surveyed the landscape and took in as many details as he could about the farm that spread out around them. As far as he could see in every direction, there was open land, divided only by the white wooden fence and the single dirt road they were driving on. At the top of a short hill, Joe came to a collection of buildings, all painted a warm yellow, the color of straw, and trimmed in dark green. The only exception was a one-story stone ranch house with tall glass windows.

As Joe pulled into the circular central drive of the farm complex, Frank ducked down in the back seat, out of sight.

A moment later Joe stopped the car, and a group of five men came walking out of the largest barn. They were all wearing jeans, T-shirts or work shirts, and boots. The man leading them was older than the rest. His nose was bent, probably from being broken a couple of times, Joe thought.

"Stay down," Joe said, under his breath to Frank. "A welcoming committee is on its way."

"Good luck," Frank said.

Joe got out of the car and walked forward slowly as the five men came toward him.

"Boys," the leader said over his shoulder to the group behind him, "looks like we're going to have to make that sign at the gate bigger. This guy missed it somehow." When he smiled, four gold teeth showed in front. "My name's Taper. I'm foreman at Wind Ridge, just so you know what I say goes. I'm going to say this once. Climb back in your car. You're trespassing."

"I'm not trespassing," Joe said. "I'm looking for a job."

"Not interested," the man said before Joe had finished his sentence.

He seems to be in a hurry to get me off the ranch, Joe thought. "But you don't know what I can do," Joe said aloud.

The man with the gold teeth said, "I know you can't hear very well. And you don't look like you ever worked on a ranch before."

"No," Joe said, trying to sound as confident as he could. "But I only have to be shown something once. Don't you need any help? I'll do anything."

Taper licked his dry upper lip, while he sized Joe up. "Can't help you. Mr. Barnell does his own hiring," he said finally.

"All right. Where is he? Can I talk to him?"

Taper looked away from Joe. "I don't think he's here right now."

He's the foreman, Joe thought to himself, and he doesn't know if Barnell's here? His nose is going to grow if he keeps saying things like that.

"No problem. I'll come back tomorrow," Joe said, climbing back into the car.

"Nobody invited you," said Taper.

"That's okay—my feelings aren't hurt," Joe said. He gave Taper one of his patented golden smiles, even though he didn't have any gold teeth to go with it. Then he drove away.

As soon as he was on the highway and out of sight, Joe pulled over quickly to the side of the road.

"What's going on?" asked Frank, sitting up on the backseat.

"Did you hear everything? Those guys wanted me gone yesterday," Joe said. "And I don't believe that Barnell isn't there. They're hiding something, and I'm just in the mood to go back for a look."

Frank shook his head at his impatient brother. "If you get caught, you'll never get a job there."

"I can fix that," Joe said with a grin. "I won't get caught. Let's go."

Joe left the car and hurried back to the farm on foot, with Frank following close behind. He ran along the fence, keeping low and out of sight for as long as he could. But there was nothing to hide behind between the fence and the barns.

"Run like crazy," Joe said. "And don't stop till you get to that longest barn."

They took off across the clearing and ducked along the outside of a barn large enough to house seventy horses or more. Cautiously Joe crept toward the back of the barn, ducking whenever he came to an open window that faced a stall.

He could hear horses in some of the stalls, their hooves rustling the straw.

39

Suddenly Joe stopped and signaled Frank to be quiet. "Voices," Joe whispered.

The two brothers listened as the angry remarks of two men spilled out of the stall opening just in front of them.

"I've had it with you pushing me around, Andy!" one guy was saying.

"What are you going to do, Josh?" said the other. "Quit? Cry? Call your mommy?"

"That's what you want. You want everyone to quit so you'll be the only one left. Well, forget it. Taper won't trust you any more than he does now. He knows what you've been up to."

Then Joe heard Andy give a mean laugh.

"Who's that? Who's there?" said a voice coming up behind Frank and Joe.

The brothers froze and turned slowly. Then they moved away from the open window where they had been listening. Standing behind them was an old man in neatly pressed jeans and a blue denim shirt. His sunglasses had black lenses, too dark to see out of, and his hair was white, as white as the cane he carried. "Who's there?" he asked again, tapping the wall with his cane.

"Uh, it's only us," Joe said, giving his brother a what-do-we-do-now? shrug.

"Who's us?" asked the blind man with a laugh. "Did you come with Doc Luthen, the vet?"

"Uh, yeah, right," Frank said.

40

"Well, how is Angel Eyes?" said the man. "Is she ready to be mated yet? Doc said any day now. That's why he's been out here four times a day, isn't it?"

"Oh, yeah, for sure," Joe said. Then he turned to Frank. "Well, is she ready?"

Frank looked blankly at his brother. "You saw her last," he said. "Is she?"

"Well, not really," Joe answered.

"Never mind. I'll ask Doc myself," said the blind man, turning around. He swung his cane in an arc, tapping the ground and the wall next to him as he walked away. "You two don't know whether to put your hats on your heads or on your feet."

Frank and Joe looked at each other. There was no reason to say what they were both thinking—that it had been a close one.

After that they decided not to push their luck. They scrambled back to their car before anyone else saw them.

"Well, what did we learn?" Frank asked, driving off.

"We learned that some guy there named Andy can't be trusted," Joe said. "We also learned they're waiting for a horse named Angel Eyes to be ready to be mated. And there's someone on the farm who's blind. But we scored zip about Ardyce."

Joe looked over at his brother. Frank didn't agree or disagree or even nod.

41

"Joe," Frank said in a weak voice. And that was all he said. Suddenly his hands slid off the steering wheel, and he slumped over onto the seat next to his brother.

Joe took one look and knew that Frank was out cold—out cold with his foot pressing down on the gas pedal—and the car was rocketing off the road!

5 On the Wrong Track

Joe tried not to panic, but it was hard to stay calm. His heart raced and thumped as the car bounced toward the woods. Straight ahead was a cluster of tall, thick-trunked trees coming closer and closer. If Joe didn't do something soon, he and Frank would both be splatters on the dashboard!

But with Frank slumped across him, unconscious on the seat, Joe could hardly move. He leaned over and struggled to grab the steering wheel. Could he steer the car with only one hand—and from the passenger side? Come on, Frank, get off me, Joe thought. Move!

At the last possible moment Joe turned the wheel

43

and the car swerved just in time to miss the trees. Joe strained to reach the brake pedal, then switched off the ignition. Finally he sat back on his own side of the car, sweat forming on his face and neck.

"I've heard of falling asleep at the wheel, but this is ridiculous," he muttered, making a joke to cover his concern. Then he shook his brother gently. "Frank, what's wrong?"

Slowly Frank's eyes opened. Then color began to spread across his pale face as he twitched back to life. "What happened?" Frank mumbled.

"You took a nap—while you were driving," Joe said, trying not to sound as worried as he was.

"I did?" Frank rubbed his face with both hands. "I don't remember. Maybe I bounced off that horse of McCord's harder than I thought."

"Probably. We'd better get you checked out," Joe said. He hopped out of the car and came around to the driver's side. "I'll drive, okay?"

"No argument," Frank said with a smile. He slid over and soon fell asleep, leaning his head against the passenger-side window.

When they got back to Stallion Canyon, Joe found Roger and Nina Glass playing Scrabble in the living room. Briefly Joe explained the events of the day and asked Roger whether he could recommend a good doctor.

"I sure can," Roger said, laughing. "And she

should be home any minute. My wife, Barbara, is a surgeon at Sonoma Hospital."

"That's why she's never home," Nina chimed in.

An hour later Barbara Glass arrived. She had large green eyes and curly dark hair identical to Nina's. Her smile was just the kind of reassurance Joe needed. She examined Frank's head in a bright corner of the living room while Joe talked a mile a minute about what had happened at Wind Ridge Farm.

"Well, it sounds like a minor concussion," Barbara concluded after she had heard all about the Hardys' day. "But I'm worried about the fact that you lost consciousness twice. That could be serious. I recommend bed rest for a day or two until we see how you are."

"Forget that," Frank said. "I'm on a case. Besides, I feel okay now."

"Yeah, and anyway they don't have time for bed rest, Mom," said Nina. "They have to go into the city to see Billy Morales. And I'm going with them."

"Billy? I didn't know he was still in the Bay Area," said Barbara.

"I made a bunch of phone calls this afternoon and found out where he lives," Nina said proudly. "He agreed to meet me tonight at eight o'clock in Ghirardelli Square."

"Hey, great work, tracking him down," Frank said.

"Thanks. I'm beginning to like this detective business," Nina said.

"Sorry, Nina. You can't go into San Francisco tonight," said Barbara. "I don't want you out late, especially since your father needs your help here tomorrow morning."

"Mom!" Nina looked pleadingly at her mother.

"Sorry," Barbara said firmly. "And, Frank, I don't think you should go either, with that head."

"I feel okay. How do we recognize Billy?" Frank said, turning to Nina and Roger.

"He's easy to spot," Roger told him. "He's the only adult you'll see who's four feet seven inches tall."

"Good luck," Nina called as Frank and Joe climbed into their car and headed back toward the city.

When Frank and Joe reached San Francisco, they left their car at the hotel, then took a cable car to the city's famous Fisherman's Wharf area. There they stopped for a delicious seafood dinner, then walked to Ghirardelli Square, a three-story brick building and plaza overlooking the bay. Once the building had been a chocolate factory. Now it housed a small chocolate shop and a number of colorful crafts galleries, boutiques, and restaurants.

This is a great city, Frank thought to himself as he and Joe wandered among the tourists and San

Franciscans who were all bundled up against the cold San Francisco summer night. He loved the atmosphere—people buying snacks, looking in shops, and listening to the street musicians who performed in the open air.

Every few minutes, however, Frank checked back at the elevator where Billy Morales had promised to meet Nina.

"Maybe he's not coming," Joe said.

"Maybe he is," Frank said, poking his brother and nodding toward the elevator. Standing there in white linen pants, a white shirt, a white cotton sweater, and white track shoes was a short man whose dark eyes darted nervously at everyone he saw.

Frank walked over to him. "Billy Morales?" he asked.

"Yeah," said Billy. His voice was high-pitched, and he seemed surprised at being called by his name.

"Nina Glass told us to meet you here," Joe said.

Frank watched closely and saw that the mention of Nina's name didn't make Billy more comfortable. Instead, a look of concern spread across his brow. "What's going on? Where's Nina?" he said, looking around and not at the Hardys. "She said she'd be here. She had something important to talk about."

"She wants you to talk to us," Frank said.

"Yeah, she said you'd want to help us," Joe said.

47

"Help you do what?" Billy asked.

"Find Nightmare," Frank said with careful timing. Would Billy flinch at the mention of the horse's name? Frank thought the jockey twitched slightly, but he wasn't sure.

"What are you talking about?"

"We're trying to find out who stole Nina's horse," Joe said.

Billy didn't say anything for a minute. Instead he reached into the pocket of his baggy pants and pulled out a small white mouse. "I love animals," he said, petting the tiny mouse as he held it.

Right, Frank thought. Maybe he loved Nightmare so much he wanted to keep the horse himself.

"If you cared about that horse, you'll tell us what happened the day he was stolen," Frank said calmly.

"I already told the police everything," Billy answered. "I was sick. I left the track early. That's all. I was too sick to ride."

"That doesn't make sense," said Frank. "Nina told us you once rode a horse knowing your leg was broken and needed to be set in a cast. I can't picture that kind of person dropping out of a race because he doesn't feel well."

Instead of answering, Billy turned and walked to a table at an outdoor café in the square. He sat down and took sunflower seeds from his pocket to feed his mouse. When Frank and Joe sat down with

48

him, Billy asked, "Why do you guys want to start this whole mess over again?"

Neither Hardy answered, and Billy just gazed off in the distance at the lighted boats in the water.

"People think animals are dumb," Billy said. "No way. They're smart and they know what's fair. You want to know about that horse? I'll tell you. That horse had heart. I always knew it. I mean, you didn't have to whip that horse. You didn't even have to talk to him. He could read your mind. 'Hold up. Save it. Now! Make your move. Take the inside.' And he'd just do it."

"He sounds like one terrific horse," Joe said.

"He was," Billy said with a faraway look on his face.

"So why didn't you ride him that day?" Frank asked again. "You would have won."

"No. I would have lost, and maybe I would have gotten killed," Billy said quietly.

"Killed?" Frank repeated. He glanced at his brother in surprise. Was Billy about to reveal another side to this story—something deeper and darker than they had suspected?

"Something was going on, that's all," Billy said. "Let's leave it at that."

"Did someone threaten you?" asked Frank.

Billy shook his head. "Look, why don't you guys just lay off? This is none of your business. Why do you want to stir it all up again?"

49

"You ride horses—we solve mysteries," Joe said simply. "It's just something we've got to do."

Billy nodded and put his mouse in his shirt pocket for a while.

"Okay, I'm going to tell you the truth," he said. "For Nina's sake. Because I don't want you wasting your time chasing after me or thinking I know anything about Nightmare when I don't. The truth is, a few months before the California Classic, I started getting dizzy spells. Bad ones. I tried to shake them off, but I couldn't. Then about a week before the race I was riding a three-year-old down in Kentucky, and I got a dizzy spell and fell. I wasn't hurt too bad, but I couldn't shake the fear. I couldn't stop thinking, What if it happens again, during a race? I could fall again and be trampled. It's a horrible thing, fear."

"And that's why you didn't ride Nightmare?" asked Frank.

Billy nodded. "I came in that morning to see how it would be. I started getting dizzy right there in the barn, so I left—and I've never raced since." Billy hung his head, clearly embarrassed, even now, to be telling Frank and Joe this. "It's nothing to ride with a broken leg," he added. "But once you get the fear, it's all over."

"Why didn't you tell this to the police?" Frank asked suspiciously.

"What was I supposed to say? I lost my nerve?"

Billy asked. "I had a reputation. I didn't want anybody to know that the famous Billy Morales was afraid to ride again." Billy stood up to leave. "Say hi to the Glasses for me. They're good horse people. And good luck with your mystery—although I doubt you'll ever see that horse again."

What did he mean by that? Frank wondered as he watched the jockey disappear into the crowds. When Billy was gone, Frank and Joe wandered out into the dark streets.

"Think he's telling the truth?" Joe asked as they walked. "I don't."

Frank took a deep breath of the cold, wet San Francisco night air. "Well, you know what Dad always says: 'If you're not sure a suspect's telling the truth, you're better off thinking he's lying . . . at least at first.'"

Joe stopped and looked at Frank.

"Did you hear that?" Joe asked.

"Footsteps," Frank said with a slow nod. He had a strong feeling that someone was following them. Was it Billy Morales? Or someone else?

Frank started to walk again, talking to Joe in normal tones as if he hadn't noticed. But at the same time he was listening for footsteps behind them, waiting to see if someone in the dark was going to make a move.

When they got to Lombard Street, Frank followed the cable car tracks, still trying to listen, watching for shadows from behind. A cable car was coming, its bell clanging, and the ground rumbled as the car tried to slow on the tracks.

"Want to grab this car and take a ride?" Joe asked Frank as they moved into the street.

Before Frank could answer, he felt hands on his back, pushing him hard. Frank fell forward onto the concrete—right in the path of the speeding cable car!

6 Strange Interview

Frank hit the ground, stunned, and sprawled across the cable car tracks. The cold metal rattled and vibrated against his outstretched body. For a fraction of an instant, he saw Joe lying near him. Then he heard a bell coming closer, clanging over and over, and people screaming. The cable car was roaring toward him, trying to stop inches away.

Frank rolled sideways just as the cable car squealed to a stop.

The next thing he knew, hands were pulling him up. A crowd of people—passengers from the cable car—had jumped off to see if he was all right. Their voices were a blur.

"Are you all right?" Frank heard the loudest voice ask. Then he saw the cable car conductor pushing his way through the crowd. The conductor was at least six and a half feet tall, almost too big for the cable car. He leaned into Frank's face, looking worried.

"Where's my brother?" Frank mumbled, standing up shakily.

"I don't know anything about your brother," the conductor said. "I just saw you—and some guy pushing you."

"What guy?" Frank demanded. "What did he look like? Where did he go?"

"I don't know. Kind of tall. Curly hair, blond maybe, hard to tell under the streetlights. He was wearing jeans and a denim jacket. It had a big rip down one sleeve."

"And you didn't see where he went?" Frank asked again, rubbing his head. The conductor shook his head.

"Hey, Frank!"

Frank turned and saw Joe coming toward him, rubbing his shoulder but grinning just the same.

"You all right?" Frank asked.

"Yeah. But someone *was* following us, Frank. I got pushed," Joe said.

"Me, too," Frank said.

"I don't know what you guys are up to or who your enemies are," the conductor said. "But you'd better be careful. And I'll tell you something else. If I were you, I'd watch my back."

* * *

By eleven o'clock Frank and Joe were back in their hotel room, and Joe was calling their father in Los Angeles. Joe told him all about the case they were working on, and that they might not join him as soon as they had planned.

Then they tried to get some sleep, but Joe couldn't calm down. He couldn't stop thinking about the "accident" in front of the cable car.

"It could have just been some nut who likes to push people in front of cable cars," Joe said, eating nachos and drinking a strawberry milk shake he had ordered from room service.

"Sure, random violence is a possibility," Frank said. "But it's not likely. I think it's got something to do with the fact that we're looking for Nightmare. A lot of people know we're on the case—and someone doesn't like it."

"Maybe someone like Billy Morales?" Joe suggested.

"He's the logical suspect," Frank agreed. "And he could have followed us easily. But do you really think he's big enough to push us both into the street?"

"You're right," Joe said. "So who?"

Frank shrugged. "I don't know. Could be anyone —someone from McCord's ranch or from Wind Ridge. We'll just have to wait until he shows his face again. In the meantime, take the conductor's advice. Watch your back."

* * *

In the morning, Frank and Joe drove out to Wind Ridge Farm so Joe could go under cover as a stable hand—*if* they'd hire him.

"I'll call you or find a ride back," Joe told his brother. "You'd better not wait around. That'll look suspicious."

Frank nodded. "I'm going to spend the day doing some research of my own," he said with a mysterious smile. He gave his brother a thumbs-up sign, for good luck, and drove off.

As soon as Joe arrived at the big barn, Taper appeared.

"I thought I told you not to bother coming back," Taper said with his angry twang.

"I really need a job," Joe answered, trying to sound humble.

For a moment Taper gave Joe a sidelong stare. Then he shrugged and led Joe into the stone ranch house with its tall windows. Joe noticed there were television monitors in almost every room. Security really is tight, he thought. What do they have to hide?

Taper held open a door to a room where classical music was playing on a stereo. The room was a modern office with a wall of monitors—about a dozen of them. Each one captured a view of some part of the farm. Joe saw himself on two of them.

"Mr. Barnell," Taper said, "this young fella is looking for a job."

Joe stepped into the room and immediately thought to himself, This is not your ordinary horse farm owner.

Bill Barnell was a fifty-year-old man with clean, smooth skin and soft, wavy brown hair. He was standing on an artificial grass putting green, wearing bright red Bermuda shorts, a safari jacket, a baseball cap, and snakeskin cowboy boots. He was practicing his putting, swinging in rhythm to the music. He didn't look as if he'd ever worked hard in his life.

Barnell didn't look at Joe. He just kept hitting golf balls. "What do you know about him, Mr. Taper?"

"I know that he's breathing, Mr. Barnell, and that's about it."

"Is he smart, Mr. Taper? You know I have strong views on the subject."

Taper looked at Joe with a smile. "Well, he's got his shoes on the right feet, Mr. Barnell."

"Have you explained my views on the subject, Mr. Taper?"

Taper spoke quietly to Joe. "Mr. Barnell doesn't hire anyone who's *too* smart."

Barnell stopped putting long enough to say, "I insist that my hands work hard. But that never involves thinking, asking questions, or formulating ideas or plans. Understood?"

Joe nodded. Maybe Taper and Barnell thought

that meant he agreed. But, he thought, The man's got to be hiding something in plain sight. That's why he wants guys who are so dumb they can't see.

"Do we need him?" Barnell asked.

"We lost a stable hand this morning, Mr. Barnell."

Barnell looked over—not at Joe or Taper, but at a monitor that showed Joe and Taper. "This is a brood-mare farm, son. A lot of people pay me a bucket of money to take care of their horses. I stable 'em, feed 'em, and get 'em ready to be mated. You've got to treat them as if they were your brother. Do you have a brother, son?"

"No," Joe said quickly.

Barnell frowned. "Drawing conclusions is a sign of intelligence, son. Don't disappoint me." Barnell pulled a portable phone from his back pocket and began making a call. The interview was obviously over.

When Joe and Taper were outside again, in the warm sunlight, Taper called to a red-haired guy about twenty years old, wearing faded jeans that were covered with mud and bits of hay. His white T-shirt had the sleeves rolled high to expose his biceps. He jogged over, chewing a large wad of gum.

"Andy, new stable hand."

Andy looked at Joe as if he were seeing a new species of slime.

"I'm Joe. How's it going?" Joe said.

58

Andy ignored the question. "I'll show you the locker room first" was all he said.

As they walked across the lawn to one of the smaller buildings, Joe thought, This is the same guy Frank and I overheard yesterday, right before the blind man spoke to us. Andy—young guy, tough voice, bad attitude. The one who can't be trusted.

Andy opened the door to the locker room and went in, almost letting the door hit Joe in the face.

"You put your stuff in here at five in the morning, and you don't set foot back in here till five in the afternoon," Andy said. Joe looked around at the rows of tall metal lockers and wondered if any of them held a denim jacket with a torn sleeve.

But Andy was on the move, and they were back outside in about fifteen seconds. Then Andy took Joe to the stable.

"Beautiful horses," Joe said, as they walked from stall to stall.

"You won't think they're so beautiful after you clean up for a week," Andy said with a laugh. "Let's get to work."

They both picked up pitchforks and began to muck out stalls, taking out the old straw and tossing in the new. About every five minutes, Andy walked by to check on Joe.

"The straw has to be thicker. And you've got to put the water bucket in exactly the same place every time or that horse will freak."

59

"Okay. Thanks," Joe said, trying to give Andy a friendly smile.

Joe lifted the water bucket to move it, but just then Andy stuck out his pitchfork and Joe tripped. The water spilled all over the clean straw.

Andy laughed. "Well, looks like you have to put down fresh straw and start all over again," he said.

"Just get off my case," Joe said. "You tripped me on purpose."

"Prove it," Andy said with a sneer.

"What's his problem?" Joe asked a short, friendly-looking guy who had introduced himself as Josh Lieber when Andy walked away.

"He does that to every new hand who comes along," Josh said, pushing his black hair off his forehead. "He's trying to keep you down, so Taper won't favor you. He has big dreams of being Taper's assistant foreman someday."

"Strange way to shoot for a promotion," Joe said.

Josh just shook his head.

For the rest of the morning Joe tried to stay out of Andy's way. But everywhere he went, Andy was right behind him.

Great, Joe thought. How am I supposed to snoop around or find Julian Ardyce or find out *anything* with him dogging me all the time?

Finally, late in the afternoon, Joe found his chance to slip away. He headed back to the locker room. Inside, he started at one end and worked his way down, opening every locker. He was looking for a denim jacket with a torn sleeve, and he almost hoped he'd find it in Andy's locker. But then he remembered what the cable car conductor had said: the guy who pushed them was a blond. Andy had red hair.

Halfway down the first row, Joe heard the door behind him open. Quickly, he squeezed into a locker and closed the door.

Joe could hear slow footsteps on the tile floor, walking right in front of the locker he was in.

"Joe? You in here?" It was Andy.

Finally the footsteps left. Quickly Joe climbed out and checked the rest of the lockers, listening for the door to open again. But he found nothing—no torn denim jacket, no clues.

There's got to be something, Joe thought, as he stopped outside the locker room. He bent over to tie his shoes, and that's when he saw it—a set of footprints in the muddy ground. He knelt to examine them closely. Left boot . . . right boot . . . hole. Left boot . . . right boot . . . hole. This is it! Joe thought. The holes were small, almost perfectly round indentations in the soil. Just the size of the tip of a cane—or a gold-handled horse-head walking stick!

It was 4:20 P.M. when Joe came back to the main barn.

"You're late," Andy called, then came over to

61

check his work. "And you're filling the feed troughs too full. The horses are going to spill a lot of oats all over the floor when they eat."

"Okay," Joe groaned. He started to empty some of the feed into a pail, but Andy grabbed the pail away.

"Look, smart guy, that's not the way it's done. I showed you five times."

Joe couldn't take it any longer. "If you want to ride something, try a horse—but get off my back," he said, turning around to face Andy.

Andy slowly raised his fists in front of him and came closer to Joe.

"Hey, I don't want to fight," Joe said.

"I'm not giving you a choice," Andy said, taking the first swing.

7 Over the Edge

Joe ducked just as Andy's powerful fist came flying toward his face.

Instinctively, Joe put up his defense. But he didn't take a swing or even move. Just what I don't need, Joe thought. Something to call attention to me and get me kicked out of here, *fast*.

Suddenly, without warning, Andy swung again, this time coming closer. The punch caught Joe in the chest, and Joe's famous temper flared hot and red.

"Okay, sucker, you're dead meat!" Joe said. He sidestepped Andy and then whirled around, whipping his elbow in an arc that nailed Andy right above the belt line.

Andy gasped and almost spit his lungs out. "I can't breathe!" He coughed as he doubled over.

Joe pushed him down in the straw. In an instant, he was sitting on Andy's chest, grabbing a handful of shirt in one tightly clenched fist.

"Now get off my case—understand?" yelled Joe.

"What's going on here?"

Joe looked up. Mr. Taper was standing in the door of the stall with his arms crossed against his chest. Three other men were standing behind him.

"This isn't a boxing ring. We've got serious work to do around here," Taper said. Sunlight made his gold teeth gleam. "Pack up your things, Joe."

Joe pounded the straw with his fist. Why hadn't he controlled his temper? If he got thrown out of there now, he'd never be able to solve this case.

Joe knew he had to do something fast, even if it meant apologizing to Andy. "Mr. Taper, I'm sorry. Don't fire me. It won't happen again."

But the foreman shook his head. "Sorry, kid. I won't put up with any trouble."

"Ahhhh, Taper, you've got it all wrong," said one of the men behind the foreman. Joe looked up and recognized him. It was the old blind man he'd run into during his first visit to Wind Ridge. "It wasn't the new boy's fault. Andy's been giving him the spurs all day. I think he took about all a fella should take."

"Is that true?" Taper asked Andy.

"I was breaking him in," Andy said. "He's green,

and I thought you wanted me to show him the ropes."

Taper thought for a minute. "If this happens again, you'll both be out of here," he said.

Just then a hand came running into the barn, yelling for Taper. "It's Angel Eyes. Doc says she's ready."

"All right. All right. I hear you."

Joe saw Taper's eyes dart around to him, almost as if he didn't want Joe to hear the conversation.

Taper hurried out of the barn, shouting orders. "Andy, hook up a trailer for me, pronto. I'll tell Mr. Barnell."

"What's going on?" Joe asked Josh Lieber, who was standing nearby.

"Doc must think Angel Eyes is ready to be mated," he answered. "So we're taking her over to a stud farm."

"Where?" Joe asked.

"Uh, how should I know?" answered Josh, and he rushed off.

Joe had the strange feeling that Josh had changed his answer before he spoke.

Outside the barn, Joe watched Andy hook up a horse trailer to the back of a yellow truck that said Wind Ridge Farm in dark green letters on the door.

Bill Barnell and Taper were off to one side by themselves, talking and watching a chestnut mare being walked into the trailer.

65

Then Taper went over to give the trailer and the horse one final check.

Joe strolled up to him. "What's the hurry?" he asked.

"These things have to be handled quickly," Taper said, giving Joe a smile.

"Where are you taking her?" Joe asked.

Taper scowled. "Do your job and mind your business—that's what we pay you for. Is that clear?" Then Taper walked away.

Yeah, clear as mud, Joe thought. Friendly one minute, angry the next. All I asked was where was he going. That pushed a real hot button. Maybe I'd better see for myself what the secret is, Joe decided.

Joe moved casually to the back of the trailer that held Angel Eyes. It was a standard single-horse trailer—open in back above the short half doors. Anyone who was watching would think Joe was just patting the horse's rump. But out of the corner of his eyes, Joe was really checking in every direction.

This is crazy, Joe thought to himself, and I'm probably going to get killed. But here goes!

As soon as he was sure no one was watching, he boosted himself over the door and into the trailer with the horse.

There was almost no room inside. "Calm down, Angel Eyes," Joe whispered as the horse whinnied and began to move around nervously in the tight space.

Joe scrunched down in the left rear corner of the

66

trailer, trying to stay out of her way and praying she wouldn't kick him in the head. In the next instant, the truck pulled away and Joe froze, knowing that Angel Eyes would jerk backward. She came within inches of stepping on him.

The horse snorted nervously again and stepped from side to side. Joe could tell she was becoming more and more agitated by his presence.

Come on, Joe thought. You're a good talker. Say something. Calm her down. "Yeah, I know," Joe said softly to the horse. "You're not used to company. But, listen, don't worry about me. I like horses. In fact, I'm a detective and I'm trying to find a horse. Maybe you know him. Nightmare?"

Angel Eyes tried to rear up, but she couldn't move much because she was securely tied. Instead she kicked the wall of the trailer.

Almost immediately Joe felt the truck pull over to the side of the road and stop. He heard a truck door open and footsteps coming toward the trailer. Joe ducked down and tried to flatten himself against the rear door.

"What's the matter, girl?"

It was Taper checking the horse out. Joe saw the man's hand reach into the trailer. He tested the ties on the horse and then took his hand away.

"She's okay. Let's go," Taper said, getting back into the truck.

They pulled back onto the road and drove a few more miles. Soon Joe felt the trailer slow down again. He peeked out the back of the trailer, and to his surprise, he knew where he was.

They were pulling into Buzz McCord's ranch. This was where Angel Eyes was going to be mated.

Okay, Joe thought to himself, you got into this trailer, and now it's time to get out—and fast, before they get to the farm!

He climbed up on the trailer door and waited to jump out. When he saw a spot with trees for him to hide behind and some tall grass to keep him out of sight, Joe leapt from the trailer and did a quick roll to slow his momentum. In an instant he was on his feet. He ducked behind a tree and watched as the truck approached the barns at Buzz McCord's farm.

"What—?" Joe said out loud as he saw the truck go past the main barn without stopping. The truck continued down the road, disappearing over the crest of the hill and out of sight. "What's going on? Where are they going?"

Joe started to follow the truck, running like a track star, but he couldn't keep up. Already the truck was far ahead of him, and he didn't want to be seen running across McCord's farm. He needed some help.

That was when he remembered Buzz McCord's invitation to come back and take a ride around the ranch.

He didn't say I couldn't come by myself, Joe

thought half-jokingly as he hurried toward one of McCord's barns. But his heart was pounding because he knew he was hatching a crazy scheme. Don't think of this as horse stealing, Joe told himself. Just think of it as taking a friendly ride.

The ranch was quiet, and he reached a barn without being seen. Joe figured that since it was after six o'clock most of the hands would have gone home. Inside, the barn was deserted, too. Most of the stalls were empty. Joe could see why. The horses were still out in the pasture, exercising and eating grass.

Joe ran through the barn, checking every box and stall, and finally he found one tall black stallion. A wooden plaque on the door said Blackbeard.

Oh, no! Joe thought. This is the same horse that threw Frank!

But there were no other mounts to choose from, and the trailer carrying Angel Eyes was getting away.

There was no time to saddle up. As fast as he could, Joe climbed up on the horse and took off. He knew this horse could run. He just hoped it wouldn't try to throw him the way it did Frank.

He rode the horse out of the barn and down the road toward the open hilly pastures and paddocks on the far side of Buzz McCord's ranch. His strong legs gripped the horse. Be confident—that's the key to riding this horse, Joe told himself. But it was hard riding bareback, and the horse was gradually picking up speed.

Joe looked behind him. No one was following him, yet. Maybe no one had seen him. He had to hope that was true. Now, if only he could catch up to that trailer . . .

He followed the dirt road as it went lower and lower, toward the cliffs that overlooked the Pacific Ocean. The view was magnificent, with the open sky above and a huge orange sun in the west. But as the ground became steeper and the road curved more sharply, Joe began to panic.

I'm not in control, Joe thought to himself. This horse is just running for the sheer pleasure of it, and I can't stop him.

Joe pulled on Blackbeard's mane, but that didn't have any effect. And then Joe saw what was up ahead.

The road they were on was curving again, and now it was carved out of the side of a cliff that dropped half a mile straight down to the ocean.

Fifty feet in front of them was a deep hole in the road. Two skinny boards had been laid across the ditch so that a car or trailer could cross it. But the boards weren't spaced properly for a horse's legs.

"Whoa!" Joe shouted, but the animal kept running. Then suddenly Blackbeard leapt across the open ditch!

Joe tried to hold on to the horse's neck, but his hands slipped as the stallion landed from the jump.

70

Joe felt himself losing his grip, then sliding and falling.

Joe's shoulder hit the ground, but his legs kept going. Suddenly Joe realized that he was skydiving in a free-fall—straight into the Pacific Ocean below!

8 Hunted!

From above, the fall had looked to Joe like a straight drop down the cliff and into the ocean. Actually, the slope was more gradual, so Joe hit the ground about ten feet from the edge of the road.

At first, he glided down the sheer, grassy cliffside as if he were sledding on a steep slope of snow. Then as he tumbled over he hit a stone—a sharp one that caught him right in the stomach and started him bumping painfully downward.

Stones, dirt, grass, and brambles tore at his skin and ripped his clothing as he rolled over them.

I've got to slow down! Joe thought frantically, because this cliff is going to drop off sooner or later.

He grabbed at the grass, kicking and clawing at

the ground to slow himself down. Finally he landed hard on a ledge and lay there breathless in a heap as a shower of dirt and stones rained down on him.

When it was finally quiet, Joe spit the dirt out of his mouth and rolled over on his back. He looked up to where the road was and saw he had fallen a couple of hundred feet. The climb back up wasn't going to be easy, especially with the scrapes and bruises that now covered his hands and body.

"That horse is bad news," Joe said out loud. Then he laughed at his understatement.

He tried standing up. "Two bloody arms— check. Two sore legs—check. Everything battered but in working order—check," he said, trying to keep his sense of humor. His legs were shaky, his blue jeans were torn, and the polo shirt he was wearing had big holes in it, a couple of them fringed with his blood. "Frank's never going to lend me another shirt as long as I live," Joe said aloud, and laughed again.

The laughing helped. It proved he was still alive and not just a little blood-ball splash on the rocky shore below.

Joe started the long climb up the hill. Of course he knew his horse was probably back at the barn by then, and someone had probably noticed that the horse had been "borrowed." Which might mean that somebody would come looking to see who had done the borrowing. And what about Taper and the trailer? Where had they taken Angel Eyes? There was no chance of catching up with them, especially now that darkness had fallen.

The moment Joe reached the road, he heard a sound coming from the direction of McCord's barns. It was a truck, coming fast. Were they looking for him? Quickly he ducked behind a tree, just below the level of the road, and crouched low, hoping he was well hidden.

A pickup truck came down the road with its high beams blazing. A roof-mounted searchlight scanned the road and the woods on either side. As the truck rounded a curve, Joe could see several men in the back of the truck, sweeping the area with bright flashlights.

How many of them were there? Joe couldn't tell. He was too far away, and the light was fading. Two points in his favor. But even without seeing or hearing the men, Joe could tell what they were doing. They were looking for the intruder who had stolen the horse. They were hunting him!

At least they don't have any dogs, he thought to himself.

That's when the barking started to come from the cab of the pickup.

Joe knew he could have hidden from men with flashlights. But the dogs made it a very different story.

Joe licked his finger and held it in the air to check the wind direction. Good—the wind was blowing

74

from the east. That meant his scent was blowing *away* from the dogs, not toward them. A third point in his favor.

Joe had just started to move away from his tree when he saw headlights coming up the road from the other direction. In the dim light that remained, he saw that it was the Wind Ridge truck—the one that had pulled the horse trailer. It was coming back alone, without the trailer or Angel Eyes.

The Wind Ridge truck stopped on the narrow road and killed its engine. So did the pickup. Both drivers got out and met in the middle of the crossing headlight beams. Joe lay down on his stomach and scooted close enough to hear.

"Evening, Mr. McCord."

"How's it going, Taper?"

Joe strained his ears to catch every word.

"Everything's fine down the hill," Taper said. "You boys look like a hunting party."

"Horse thief," McCord said coldly. "Someone tried to run away with Blackbeard. One of my hands saw him."

"Well, one thing's for sure. The thief likes a challenge. That horse is a handful."

"The thief didn't keep him," McCord said. "The horse came back. Now we're after the fool who tried it. The tracks lead in this direction."

"My boys and I will be happy to help you find him," Taper said.

Joe didn't wait to hear more. He slid down the

cliffside until he came to some trees that would cover him. Then he ran in the direction of McCord's ranch. When he was far enough away from the two trucks, he climbed back up to the road and ran as fast as he could toward the gate.

I've got to cover ground fast before they double back, he thought. He was losing the light entirely, but it wasn't safe to run on the road that led to the barns. He cut across a pasture, trying to set a steady pace, and hoped his sense of direction would take him to the main road.

When he finally reached the highway, Joe stopped running and put his thumb out to hitch a ride. The first few cars passed him by. Finally a big, beat-up old Lincoln pulled off the road and stopped next to Joe.

The driver was a guy with long hair and a thin mustache. Although it was dark, he was wearing sunglasses. He took one look at Joe, his face scratched and muddied, his clothes torn. "Great outfit, dude," the guy said, swinging the heavy door open for Joe. "Going to a hit-and-run party?"

"Uh, my horse threw me," Joe said, climbing in and easing his bruised body down on the torn but soft seat. "Can you get me to a telephone?"

"No problem," said the driver, flipping his hair out of his sunglasses. He pounded on the dashboard hard enough to make the glove compartment pop open. Inside was a car phone. "Help yourself, dude," he said with a loud laugh.

Joe dialed the hotel and asked for his room.

"Hello," said a gruff voice.

"Frank?" Joe asked.

"Who's this?" the voice said.

"Joe. Is Frank there?"

"Uh, you got the wrong room, bud."

The guy hung up. Strange, Joe thought. He knew he had asked for the right room. Maybe the operator had misconnected him.

Joe tried again, and this time no one in the room answered. Next he called the Glasses' home, where he found Frank.

Half an hour later, Frank pulled into the gas station where Joe had been dropped off.

"What happened to you?" Frank said, eyeing Joe up and down.

"Just about everything," Joe answered.

As Frank drove them back to San Francisco, Joe filled his brother in on his day at Wind Ridge Farm: seeing Barnell, cleaning out every stall, fighting with Andy, then hiding in the trailer and going to Buzz McCord's ranch, where he got thrown from the black horse.

"But I picked up a real clue today," Joe said, saving the best for last.

"I *knew* you were holding out on me! What?"

"Some footprints in the mud," Joe explained. "Two boot prints with a small round hole beside them. As though a heavy man had been there with a walking stick or cane."

"Ardyce!"

"Right."

"That's great," Frank said. "But it's circumstantial evidence—lots of people could have canes. How about a little word that begins with *P* and ends with *F*—proof."

"I'll get the proof tomorrow," Joe said. "Meanwhile, don't forget about Angel Eyes. They didn't take her to McCord's barn to be mated. They took her somewhere else."

"Where?"

"I don't know," Joe said. "But I bet it's someplace secret, and that makes me suspicious."

Frank was quiet for a while as they drove across the Golden Gate Bridge into San Francisco.

"Frank, what about that little word that begins with *F* and ends in *D*?" asked Joe.

"What are you talking about?"

"Food! Let's eat. I'm starving!"

Frank smiled and pulled up to a bright, fluorescent-lit all-night restaurant called Clown Alley. It was one of San Francisco's best burger places. While they ate, Joe told Frank more about his day.

"I picked up some useful information today," Joe said, working on the second half of his second burger. "Did you know that horse hair bleaches out in the sun just like human hair does? When I heard that, I thought maybe Julian Ardyce used bleach on Nightmare's leg before they took him from the track, to make him look like Spats."

78

Frank munched his burger across the little round table in the crowded restaurant.

"Could be, but it's more likely he used chalk or paint. Speaking of that, I spent the day at a racetrack," Frank said. "I watched horses go in and out. The guards check the release papers and sometimes the tattoos, but the security is loose. No one I talked to had seen Ardyce since the Nightmare robbery."

"I'm going to see him, big as life, at Wind Ridge Farm," Joe said confidently.

"That man *is* bigger than life," Frank said with a laugh. "I've got other news, too. I asked around about Danny Chaps, the groom. Someone told me he moved to Tampa, Florida, after Roger Glass fired him. After about twenty phone calls, I tracked him down."

"Great! What did he say?"

"Nothing. He hung up on me as soon as I mentioned Nightmare. And when I called back, he wouldn't answer. I think he was involved in the robbery. I think someone paid him to go off and buy a soft drink while Nightmare was being stolen. And I think someone is paying him to stay lost and keep quiet about the robbery now."

"Doesn't sound like we'll get much more out of him," Joe said.

After they finished their burgers, Joe and Frank went back to their hotel room.

Frank unlocked the door, and Joe reached for the

light switch just inside the room. But the light didn't come on.

"I'll turn on another one," Joe said, stepping into the room.

But as he crossed the room in the darkness, Joe heard a sound that made his heart skip a beat. Someone was in there! In the next instant he felt a sharp pain on the back of his head. Then he heard Frank cry out and fall.

Someone's been waiting in my bed, Joe thought as he slumped to the floor, unconscious.

9 In Deep Water

The first thing Frank heard when he woke up was water gently slapping against a shore. In his half-dream, Frank almost thought he could feel the water licking at his toes. It felt icy cold for just a second, and then it was gone.

That's strange, Frank thought. Water . . . and a dull ache in the back of my head. How long has it been there, that dull ache?

Then he remembered. Ever since he was hit from behind!

Frank's eyes popped open. Slowly he began to piece together what had happened. He and Joe had walked into their hotel room, and—blam!—they had been hit on the head. Frank reached for the lump on his head, but he couldn't move his arms. His hands were tied at the wrists, stretched above his head. His feet were also tied to something, but it was too dark to see what it was.

The cold water touched his feet again—and Frank realized that he was outside and it was night. The air was damp and chilly. He was tied with his feet near water.

"Joe!" Frank cried, struggling against the ropes.

Frank heard a grumble and gurgle in the darkness very nearby. Joe was waking up, too.

"Huh? Wha—? What's going on? Where are we?"

A foghorn interrupted them, blasting its eerie voice through the night. Then a half-moon burst from behind thick black velvet clouds.

In the sudden moonlight, Frank could at last see that they were on a craggy shore. And he could see what they were tied to—opposite arms of a heavy iron anchor that stretched at least four feet across.

Frank craned his neck to look around and behind him. The tight ropes chewed into his wrists and ankles as he twisted, but he had to see where they were. Behind and beyond them was a building—an ominous, cold, deserted building with towers and turrets encircled by barbed-wire fences and barricades.

"Joe!" Frank gasped. "I know where we are! Look out at the water. See the lights? That's San Francisco. We're on Alcatraz Island!"

"Frank, the water," Joe said. His voice came in short stabs because he was so cold. "The tide's coming in."

"I know," Frank said. "If we don't get loose, we're going to drown!"

"Oh, no," Joe moaned. "I should have known. This is all my fault."

"Give me a break," Frank said. "It's not your fault."

"No, listen. I just remembered. Before I called you at the Glasses'," Joe said, "I called our hotel room. Someone answered and said I had the wrong room. But I had the *right* room—and two guys were waiting there for us for hours! They socked us the minute we walked in."

Frank didn't want to think about who had knocked them out or, worse, who had sent them to do it. Not now. There were more important problems to deal with—and fast.

"The water's rising quickly," Joe said.

"I know." Frank tried to rub his hands against the metal anchor. But the water was so cold he almost couldn't feel his hands.

Frank could hear Joe grunting and groaning, straining to loosen the ropes. An oversize wave suddenly came up and momentarily covered Frank with water. When it receded, he gasped for air.

"Hang on," Joe called. "I got my feet free."

"Way to go," Frank said, spitting salt and sand out of his mouth.

83

A moment later, Joe was able to slide his tied hands toward the other side of the anchor, closer to Frank's hands. Frank felt his brother's fingers dig at the rope around Frank's wrists. Finally the rope loosened, and Frank pulled his hands free.

It only took a few more minutes to untie Joe's hands and Frank's feet. Then, moving as quickly as their cold bodies could, they helped each other scale the tall stones and climb away from the water.

Frank collapsed on a dirt path, leading up to the prison. A sign nearby said, See the Prison on Alcatraz. Take a Guided Tour.

"I think I'll skip the tour," Frank said exhaustedly.

While Frank rested, Joe scoured the landscape for bits of trash and scrap paper. He was gone almost twenty minutes, but when he came back he was smiling.

"Look what I found. Matches! I had to go through a grungy garbage can to find them," Joe said, walking back toward shore. He washed his hands in the water, then came back to Frank and lit a small trash fire.

"Do you think the Coast Guard will see the fire?" Frank asked as he warmed his hands over it.

"We'll keep building it till they do," Joe said. "I've got plenty of matches."

About an hour later, a Coast Guard cutter pulled up to the island, and a crewman arrested Frank and Joe for trespassing on government property.

"No problem," Frank told the arresting guardsman. "Best news I've heard all day. Can we go someplace dry and warm now?"

The coastguardsmen took the brothers back to their station. During the trip Frank and Joe introduced themselves as detectives working on a case and explained how they had ended up at Alcatraz.

The station house was small, but it was warm. Frank and Joe, still wrapped in blankets, sat on a bench facing a telephone and called their father in Los Angeles. As he dialed the phone, Frank explained to the captain of the Coast Guard cutter that his father was a former police officer turned private investigator.

"Dad," Frank said, as soon as his father answered the phone.

"Frank? It's four o'clock in the morning." A sleepy Fenton Hardy yawned.

"Dad, we're on a speakerphone, and we're calling from a Coast Guard station," Joe said.

Mr. Hardy cleared his throat. "Well, you certainly have my interest, Joe. What's up?"

"Dad, we were arrested on Alcatraz Island," Frank said.

"Yeah, some guys knocked us out and hung us out to drown," Joe interrupted.

Then a man who looked like a steel girder in a khaki uniform—tall, straight, and strong—stepped up to the speakerphone. "Mr. Hardy. This is Captain Kulik, United States Coast Guard. Can you verify that these are your sons and vouch for their story?"

"Captain," Fenton Hardy said in a very serious voice, "in less than a minute I can have references from the FBI, the CIA, or the Pentagon. Do you want to take your choice?"

"No, sir," said the captain. "We've just completed a check on you. Thank you for your time."

"Boys," said Mr. Hardy, "call me later and fill me in on the case. It sounds like it's getting out of control."

"We'll be careful, Dad," Frank assured him.

Then the Coast Guard captain called Roger Glass for a second corroboration. Once he was satisfied, he let Frank and Joe go. It wasn't until eight that morning that Frank and Joe arrived back at their hotel.

They walked slowly through the bright lobby bustling with tourists eager to get an early start.

Frank leaned on the front desk, smiling at the young man who stood behind the reception counter. The man was in his thirties, with thick glasses and a tight-collared shirt and tie. His name tag said Harold Conifer. Service is my middle name.

"Strange middle name," Joe commented.

"May I help you?" Harold asked.

"We need a key to our room," Frank said.

Harold looked at Frank's ragged appearance with suspicion.

"What room would that be?" Harold asked.

86

"Eight seventy-three," Joe said.

Harold tapped the keys on his computer. "Names, please."

"Frank Hardy and Joe Hardy," answered Frank.

Harold tapped more keys. Then he cocked his head to one side. "Sorry. You're not registered in this hotel."

Frank's eyebrows shot up in surprise.

"Harold," Joe said. "We've been through some ugly scenes since last night, and now I want to get some sleep. Check the computer again."

"Sorry," Harold said. "The computer doesn't list you among our guests."

"Does the computer list you as a victim of assault and battery?" Joe snarled.

"Take it easy," Frank warned his brother. "Harold, you're making a mistake. We've been staying here for three days."

Harold tapped more keys. "Oh, yes, the computer indicates that."

"That's more like it," Joe said, slapping the counter with his hand.

"But," continued Harold, "you were checked out last night. I handled it myself. Someone came, paid your bill, packed up your belongings, and left. You don't have a room here anymore."

10 Up, Up, and Away

Joe couldn't believe his ears. Did part of his brain freeze when he and Frank almost drowned in San Francisco Bay? "Run that by us one more time, will you, Harold?" Joe said to the hotel desk clerk.

"I remember it clearly," said Harold, taking off his glasses to clean the lenses. "Just when I was coming on duty, around midnight, a man said that he was your uncle, that he had visited you earlier, and that he was going to check out for you. He paid your whole bill."

"Did he pay with a credit card?" Frank asked.

Joe knew what his brother was getting at: a credit-card payment meant a name and a signature—a way of tracking the guy down.

"No, he paid with cash," Harold said. "Then I

gave him the key, and he and the other man went up to collect your things."

Joe had about two dozen questions in his mind, but he couldn't decide which one to ask first. "What other man? What did they look like? What were they wearing?"

Harold held up his hands. "Guys, guys," he said. "I don't remember what they looked like. I see a thousand people a day. Who pays attention?"

"Well, how about giving us our room back so we can get some rest?" Frank said, pulling out his wallet.

"Uh, sorry, guys," said Harold. He looked a little guilty. "We're full. Not a vacant room in the house. There's a convention in town."

Joe slumped on the reception counter. "Unbelievable," he moaned. "No room. No clothes. No suitcases—no fair."

"There's only one hotel I know of that's not full," said Harold. "Right down the street. It's cheap, but I'd advise you to buy a flea and tick collar before you check in."

Frank motioned Joe to follow him away from the reception desk.

"Where are you going?" Joe asked.

"To find a phone to call the Glasses," Frank said. "Maybe they'll let us stay with them."

Joe heard more than just exhaustion in Frank's voice. "What's wrong, Frank?" Joe said.

"Think about what's happened, Joe," Frank said.

89

"Somebody knew who we were and knew where we were staying. How serious do you think they are if they left us to drown on Alcatraz Island and then tried to remove every bit of physical evidence that we were ever in this hotel?"

"You're right. Let's give Nina a call," Joe said. "Maybe we can get some sleep and then start putting this case together."

Nearly two hours later, Joe and Frank pulled up at Stallion Canyon. Nina hurried out to greet them.

"Hi," she said. "Wow! You guys look awful. I guess you really want some sleep, huh? You can crash in our foreman's trailer. He's gone for a few days. And I got one of our hands to lend you some of his clothes."

"That's great. Thanks," Frank said.

"Are you hungry?" Mr. Glass called from behind the screen door.

"Did I hear the magic words?" Joe said. He walked directly from the car to the breakfast table.

"What happened to you?" asked Barbara Glass. She was seated at a table covered with plates of pancakes, bacon, fruit, and potatoes.

Joe filled a plate and started eating. "Frank tells the story better than I do," he said.

"You just don't want to break stride while you're eating," Frank said.

Joe laughed at his brother and popped a strip of bacon into his mouth.

By the time Frank had finished recounting the events of the past twenty-four hours, Joe had finished his second helping of pancakes and was feeling almost full. A few hours' sleep and he would be ready for anything.

After breakfast, the Hardys slept in the foreman's trailer until the middle of the afternoon. They woke, took hot showers, and got dressed in a real horse-farm hand's work clothes.

Joe left the trailer first, combing his wet blond hair as he walked across the yard. Halfway across, he noticed Nina sitting on top of a fence surrounding a horse exercise ring.

"Hi, Nina," Joe greeted her, smiling. "Is there anything to eat around here?"

"I don't believe you're hungry again!" Nina said with a laugh. "You can eat at the party."

"What party?" asked Frank.

"Our neighbors at the ranch next door are having a party," Nina said. "We're invited, and they said we should bring you. Mom's at work, but my dad and I are leaving soon."

At five o'clock that afternoon, Joe, Frank, and Nina and Roger Glass drove over to the neighboring horse ranch, where about seventy-five people were eating barbecue, riding horses, and having a good time. In the center of a large open area was the main attraction—and nobody could miss it.

"Look at that! Totally fantastic!" Joe shouted on

seeing a gigantic red, white, and blue hot air balloon.

The balloon was tied to the ground, but every once in a while, the balloon's pilot would take several guests up for a ride around the area.

Frank and Joe got separated from the Glasses and wandered through the crowd, working their way from the barbecue to the fresh roasted ears of corn to the muffins. They ran into Buzz McCord, and then Frank saw someone else he recognized. It was the stable hand who had helped him onto the black horse at Buzz's ranch—the one who had whispered to him about Julian Ardyce.

"Hey, Joe," Frank said. "Look at that guy. He has blond hair."

"So?" Joe said.

"I wonder if he also has a denim jacket with a torn sleeve," Frank said.

"Good question," Joe said. "I'll keep an eye on him."

For another half hour, Frank and Joe circulated and tried to find out whether anyone had any leads to Ardyce or Nightmare, with no success.

"We're not getting anywhere with the case," Joe said. "So let's have some fun. Let's check out the hot air balloon."

The balloon was a couple of stories high, and it billowed out as a fat, blue gas flame from a burning jet pumped it full of hot air. Joe and Frank walked around the basket of the balloon. The basket was

small. It covered an area about four feet square—
not a very large space to ride in.

"You guys want to go for a spin?" asked the pilot.
He was standing by the gas jet, adjusting the flame.

"Count me in," Joe said, immediately climbing
over the side of the basket.

Frank followed and stood on the opposite side.

"Well, I'll just go get me another lemonade," said
the pilot, "and then we'll launch this little birdie."
The pilot climbed out of the basket and turned
around to the Hardys. "Don't go away," he said
with a laugh before he disappeared into the crowd.

Joe and Frank checked out the lightweight ropes
connecting the basket to the balloon. The passengers were the heaviest thing on board.

Suddenly the basket pitched to one side, and
Frank was sent bumping into Joe and knocking him
down. Then the other side bounced.

"Hey, watch where you're stepping," Joe said.

But Frank wasn't looking at Joe. He was looking
up, and his eyes were getting wider.

"Joe. We're launched!" Frank said.

Joe stood up, looked around, and saw that they
were gently rising from the ground. All of a sudden
the top of a nearby barn was at eye level, and then it
quickly drifted below them.

"Whoa!" Joe said. "Where's the pilot?"

Frank pointed down to the ground.

People were yelling and running under the balloon, following its path, but they couldn't keep up.

93

"Do you think there's a portable phone on board?" Joe joked. "Just asking."

For the next minute the brothers didn't speak. They watched the earth beneath them spread out. They held on to the support ropes as the balloon swung freely through the air. The only sound they heard was the wind.

"Look," Joe said, lifting a rope that was dangling over the edge of the basket. "It's been cut. Someone cut us loose on purpose."

"Okay," Frank said, snapping into action. "This is going to be all right. I read an article in a magazine about how to fly one of these. To go higher, you turn up the heat in that gas jet."

"That's a good thing to know," Joe replied, pointing, "because we're about to smash into some trees!"

Frank ran to the controls and turned the lever that increased the flame. The trees were coming closer, and the wind seemed to want to blow the balloon right into them. Slowly the balloon began to rise—just in time to clear the clump of trees.

"Not bad," Joe said. "Got any suggestions for getting this thing down?"

Frank smiled slyly. "Are you in a big hurry?"

"No," Joe said, shaking his head. "Let's check out the scenery."

"I'll show you how to set the balloon down when we find a clear spot to land," Frank said.

A soft breeze blew through Frank's hair as they drifted over the hillsides of the northern California communities, not knowing where they were, just enjoying the ride.

"Hey, look," Frank said.

Joe looked down and recognized the area immediately. "It's Buzz McCord's farm," he said. "It's got to be."

Frank squinted hard at the endless white fences and the white barns perched on the hills overlooking the ocean below. What a vantage point, Frank thought, as they drifted silently on, heading north.

"What's that?" Frank asked, pointing toward a grove of trees.

Joe didn't see anything at first except trees surrounded by open pasture. But as the balloon passed directly over, he saw what looked like a small barn, tucked away from all the other buildings on the farm. It was hidden in a valley at the end of a long road that wound through Buzz's ranch.

"What's that doing on McCord's farm?" Joe said. But then he shouted, "Frank!"

Joe saw it first, but he knew his brother saw it just an instant later. Out of the barn below ran a black horse. It galloped and then trotted around the perimeter of the fenced area.

"A black horse—all by itself," Joe said, excited.

"Maybe, just maybe, it's Nightmare!" Frank said. "But we can't tell anything from here."

Joe watched the horse gallop freely through the pasture as McCord's farm disappeared smoothly behind them.

"Okay," Joe said. "Now we've got a reason to land this thing. Do your stuff, big brother."

Frank turned off a gas jet and pulled a cord that let hot air out of the balloon. It began to descend.

"Hey, too much. Too fast," Joe said.

The balloon continued to drop even after Frank let go of the cord. Joe felt himself—and the basket —tip and rock.

"We've caught some kind of downdraft," Joe said. "And there's nothing but trees here. We're going to get killed!"

"There's another ranch," Frank said, pulling the cord to make the balloon go lower again. "Maybe we can land in one of the fields."

The balloon dropped some more and caught another wind, which swept it along.

"Bring her down now!" Joe said, watching a flat field pass fifty feet, forty feet, thirty feet beneath them.

But the balloon kept skimming over the land.

"Uh-oh! We're heading for those power lines!" Frank shouted.

Joe's throat tightened at the sight of three tall, silver electrical towers standing directly in their way.

"Hold on!" Joe shouted. "We're going to be fried!"

11 On Safe Ground

Frank watched helplessly as the hot air balloon drifted straight toward the row of giant steel electrical towers and power lines that stretched out in front of them.

Frank gripped the basket of the balloon tightly. Their one hope, their one chance, was to catch another updraft that would carry them away. But it wasn't happening.

"When we get close to the lines, jump!" Joe yelled.

Frank looked over the side of the basket. "It's twenty-five feet down."

"Yeah, but for twenty-four feet, you're golden," Joe said, putting on a weak smile. "It's only the last foot you have to worry about."

Frank tried to smile, but the balloon dropped lower, and Frank's pounding heart sank with it. Now the power lines were exactly level with the basket. Twenty million volts, here we come, Frank thought. Another few seconds and they'd both be quarter-pounders.

Suddenly the basket lurched and jerked.

"An updraft!" Frank yelled.

The balloon bobbed up, carrying Frank and Joe higher.

"Climb, baby, climb!" Joe chanted.

Ever so gradually, the balloon floated over the power lines like a pole-vaulter barely skimming over the pole.

"We made it!" Joe cheered.

Then suddenly the balloon dropped straight down.

"Hold on!" Frank heard his brother shout. But Frank was already holding on with all his might.

Twelve feet, ten feet, five feet from the ground and then—*crack!* The balloon landed in the branches of an old dead tree and stuck there.

It was over. Frank didn't move until his breathing was normal again. Then he climbed out of the basket, which seemed to have survived the crash intact, and dropped the five feet to the ground. Joe followed him.

"I'm taking a survey. Which do you prefer?" Joe asked. "A runaway horse or a runaway balloon?"

"A vacation at a theme park," Frank said. "Safer rides. Where do you think we are?"

"I don't know," Joe said, "but someone does. Look." Joe was pointing toward the other end of the field in which they had landed.

At first Frank could see only a billow of dust in the distance. Then the dust cloud turned into a jeep bouncing over the hills toward them. The car screeched to a stop, and out hopped the pilot of the balloon. He was still wearing his flight jumpsuit.

"Are you guys all right? Anything broken, twisted, or bent beyond recognition?" he asked, running over to Frank and his brother.

"We're okay," Frank said.

"Yeah," Joe agreed. "How'd you find us?"

"There's always a chase team on the ground, following a balloon's flight," said the pilot. "Of course, I'm not usually in the car. I'm usually in the balloon. But I'm glad you guys are okay. Now I won't have any second thoughts about suing you!"

"Suing us?" Frank asked.

"Theft, negligence, destruction of property— those are only the highlights," said the pilot, counting off on his fingers. "Although the balloon doesn't look too bad."

Frank saw his brother's eyebrows meet. Joe was getting angry.

"Look," Joe said. "This wasn't our fault. So maybe *you* should talk to *your* lawyer first."

"Guys, I hate to interrupt your fantasy to bring you a special bulletin—but I *am* a lawyer."

"Oh," Joe said, surprised.

"We didn't steal your balloon," Frank said. "Someone cut the rope, and we can prove it. You know what a cut rope looks like, don't you?"

The pilot nodded.

"Well," Joe said, pointing up at the balloon, "there's one right up there. Check it out."

"Yeah, right. Why would someone cut the rope?"

"Because we must be getting close to a big clue and someone's getting nervous about it," Joe said.

"We're detectives working on a case," Frank explained.

The pilot laughed sarcastically. "Right, like the Hardy brothers or something?" he asked.

Frank gulped. "We *are* the Hardy brothers," he said.

The pilot slapped his forehead. "You must be kidding. Frank and Joe?" he said. "My law firm hired your father a couple of times and brought him out to San Francisco. He talked about you all the time."

After that they didn't talk about lawsuits any more. The pilot introduced himself as Tony Ludy. He asked all about the case Frank and Joe were working on and wanted to know if there was something he could do to help.

"We've got to get back to Buzz McCord's horse farm," Frank said.

"Yeah, but we have to be invisible when we do it," Joe added.

"I've got some maps you guys are going to love," Tony said, heading back to the jeep. "Chase teams have these super-detailed maps that show every road, every path, every fence, every hill and valley, so we can zero in on a balloon that's going down and get to it fast."

First Frank used a regular map of the area to point out where McCord's farm was. Then Tony brought out his detailed maps.

"McCord's farm is in the hills," Frank said.

"But the road going through the farm winds along a cliff over the ocean," Joe said. "And it's a pretty straight drop. I know because I personally ate half the dirt on that cliff when I fell down it."

"I think the secret barn is somewhere over here," Frank said. He was just making a guess, because they had flown over it so quickly.

Tony circled a section of the map with his finger. "Looks to me like you should come up from the beach. It's public access. No one can stop you."

"Walk down the beach, then climb over this hill and sneak down into the valley," Frank said, memorizing the route. "Let's give it a try."

They loaded the hot air balloon into the jeep. To Joe's amazement, the balloon folded down to a thirty-inch-square bundle. Then Tony dropped Frank and Joe at the beach, and they started walking.

Joe was the first one out of his shoes and socks, but it wasn't long before Frank, too, was feeling the pebbly sand between his toes.

"At least this way we won't leave as many tracks," Frank said. Even there, on a remote beach, Frank didn't feel entirely safe. Someone could be following them again.

Joe hopped on one foot, leaving strange footprints in the sand. "I can see your mind cranking through all the possibilities," he said to his brother. "But don't sweat the small stuff."

Frank smiled. "What's the big stuff?"

"Say we find the horse. How are we going to know if it's Nightmare?" Joe asked. "Horses don't wear name tags around their necks."

"You mean like, Hello. My name is Nightmare. If I'm stolen please return me to Nina Glass?" Frank said with a laugh. "I already thought of that. We'll check the tattoo in the horse's mouth and then tell Nina the number. If it's the same, we'll know we've found Nightmare."

"That'll be great. But what's he doing on Buzz McCord's farm? Do you think McCord and Ardyce are in this together?" Joe said.

"McCord will have to answer that one," said Frank.

Frank reached the end of the beach—the point at which they had to climb up the cliff to Buzz's property.

"No one's watching from the hill. Let's do it," Joe said.

Fun time was over. Frank slipped on his shoes and started climbing quickly.

It was a gradual climb and easy. Halfway up, Frank watched as Joe slipped through the white rail fence. Then Frank climbed in, too. Now they were on McCord's property. Frank followed the dirt road a short way down the hill and into a valley. Hidden behind trees, just the way it looked from the air, was a small stable.

"I don't get it and I don't like it," Frank complained. "Why aren't there people around? Why aren't there security cameras? Where's someone to take care of this horse?"

"This is called a lucky break," Joe said. "We get 'em sometimes, remember? So let's not waste it. Let's get over to that barn."

Frank ran quickly, ducking behind trees and checking to make sure the coast was clear before signaling Joe to come, too. Then he made the final move to the secret stable.

A fenced exercise paddock encircled the area next to the small white barn. Inside the paddock, with the entire space to itself, stood a tall black horse. It snorted out a breath nervously, obviously aware that it was being watched.

"He's beautiful," Frank said, admiring the proud animal as it moved nervously back and forth in the grassy area.

103

The two brothers climbed the fence together and slowly lowered themselves into the paddock.

"Take it easy," Joe told the horse. "We only want to look inside your mouth. Who am I kidding? *I* wouldn't be too thrilled about someone trying to look in *my* mouth."

This had to be Nightmare, Frank thought. Why else would McCord keep one horse isolated in a distant, secret barn? Frank couldn't help smiling. "Looks like we've solved another case the police couldn't," he told Joe.

"Easy, boy," Joe said, inching forward as the horse moved back toward the far side of the paddock.

The horse shook his head and whipped his tail back and forth.

Finally Joe moved close enough to pat the horse's side.

Suddenly, without warning, the horse whinnied and reared on its hind legs. Frank froze and then backpedaled as fast as he could.

"Run for the fence!" Frank shouted.

Now the horse was charging after them. Joe ran toward his brother, stumbling in the grass. Hooves thundered behind them, forcing them to keep running around the perimeter of the small fenced paddock.

Finally Frank saw his chance. He ducked under

the fence railing to safety, rolling in the grass to make sure he was clear of the wild stallion. But when he stood up and turned around, his heart nearly stopped. Joe had tripped and fallen—and the stallion was rearing up above Joe's head, ready to trample him to death!

12 Clue in the Video

"No!" Frank shouted.

He leapt over the fence, back into the paddock with the wild horse. His shout and his own wild movements were enough to distract the horse for a moment so that Joe could roll out of the way.

Without stopping, Frank ran across the paddock to the opposite fence, where he and Joe threw themselves over the white railing in identical movements, as if they were twin acrobats in the circus.

Frank and his brother sat for a moment, well away from the fenced area, catching their breath, while the horse kept whinnying and rearing angrily behind the fence.

"Let's get out of here," Joe said. "Now I know why they call that horse Nightmare!"

It was late in the evening by the time Frank and Joe returned to the Glasses' ranch. The lights were burning brightly, and smoke rose from the chimney. They had walked all the way back to Stallion Canyon from Buzz McCord's farm—about six miles. As they approached the Glasses' house, Frank could hear rhythmic rock music blasting from an open upstairs window, while classical music came from another on the first floor.

Frank knocked on the front door, and Roger welcomed them in.

Nina had apparently just taken a shower. She came into the living room, combing her wet hair. "What happened? Where'd you guys go?" she asked. "The balloon pilot came back and told us he dropped you somewhere, but he wouldn't say where. Are you okay?"

"We're okay," Joe said. "But wait till you hear about what we saw."

Then Frank told about the balloon passing over Buzz McCord's farm and about the black horse running behind the secret barn.

The hairbrush fell from Nina's hand. "A black horse?" she said, her eyes becoming pools of emotions—hope, fear, anticipation, excitement. "Was it Nightmare?"

"We don't know," Joe said, taking over the story.

107

"We went back to the farm to check the horse's tattoo. We sneaked over the fence, but we couldn't even get near him. The horse went crazy. He tried to stomp us into the ground."

"Nightmare?" Nina practically moaned. "He'd never do that. That means he hasn't been handled enough. They must not be riding him or talking to him or walking with him through the flower fields." Her face screwed up into a painful, worried expression.

"Hold on, Neen," said Mr. Glass sternly. "You don't know it's Nightmare. And I don't believe it can be."

"Why not?" Nina demanded.

Her father kept his voice calm. "Because they're saying he's on Buzz McCord's farm. I've known Buzz for twenty years, and I just don't believe he stole Nightmare. It's got to be a different horse."

"Let's go and find out," Nina said, hopping out of her chair.

"Not tonight, Neen," said Mr. Glass.

"Why not?" she practically screamed. "You just don't care!" Fighting back tears, she stormed out of the room.

A few seconds later, a door slammed deep in the house.

Mr. Glass turned to Frank and Joe. "I told you this would happen," he said. "I knew she'd get her hopes up. Now she's going to be devastated if you don't find Nightmare."

Joe shook his head. He knew exactly what Nina was feeling. If that had been his horse, he'd want to know—and right now, not tomorrow morning.

"It's not Nightmare," Mr. Glass said. "It can't be. I've been to that farm. I'd have known if Buzz was hiding something."

Joe said nothing. Frank cleared his throat. "But what if it *is* Nightmare?"

The next morning, the Hardys and Nina reached the bottom of the hill on McCord's farm at about eight-thirty and looked out toward the grove of trees that hid the small barn.

Nina didn't wait to be told this was the place. She bolted toward the exercise paddock and jumped up on the surrounding fence.

"He's not here," she moaned, jumping down.

All three of them ran for the stable door.

"Hey, wait, you guys," said Frank. He was looking around at the ground, but Nina and Joe ignored him.

"Come on," Joe said, leading Nina into the barn. They raced through the small building, checking each of the four stalls.

"Where is he?" asked Nina, standing in front of the last one.

The door was open, the stall was empty, and the floor was clean. Nina stamped the floor angrily.

Frank called from outside, "He's gone, isn't he?"

"How'd you know?" Joe answered.

"Come look out here," Frank answered. "There are fresh tire tracks. A shallow set and a deep set."

Joe could guess what the deep set meant. Someone had loaded the horse into a trailer and driven him away.

"But where'd they take him?" Nina asked.

"Who knows?" Joe said.

"Uh-oh, we've got company," Frank said.

Joe looked up and immediately recognized the truck that was coming toward them. "It's McCord."

The truck stopped, and Buzz McCord and two older ranch hands stepped out. The ranch hands had sun-dried skin and sour expressions, but Buzz's face was cold, calm, and smiling.

"Good morning," Buzz said, pushing his hat back with one finger on the brim. "You know, this is the third time you boys have come trespassing on my farm," he said. Then he laughed. "But who's counting? Hi, Nina."

Nina was silent.

"I told you two, if there was something you wanted to see or something I could do, you should ask me. You two have a way of stirring up trouble all by yourselves. Things would go a lot smoother if you'd ask for help from your friends."

"Where's the horse?" Nina asked, her voice quivering.

"We saw a horse in here yesterday," Frank said, "a black horse. Where is it?"

110

"He went home early this morning," Buzz said. "That was a mean one. Couldn't get along with anyone, man or beast. That's why I kept him down here by himself. His owner drove him away this morning, and I waved goodbye with a smile."

Nina shook her head.

"What's the matter, Nina?" Buzz asked.

"Nothing." She sniffed.

"Nina, you didn't think that black was Nightmare, did you?" Buzz asked. He looked right at Joe. "What kind of stories have you been putting in her head?"

"We saw a black horse all by itself in a secret barn," Frank said. "We don't like to let any possibility slip by."

"No, I can see that you don't," Buzz said. "I told you, Nina, if anyone's going to find Nightmare, it's going to be the Hardy brothers."

"Yeah," Nina said glumly.

Buzz's face drooped. "Say something to her, boys. I think she's starting to lose faith in you."

Joe was feeling pretty bad. "Nina, we'll find him. Don't worry."

But Nina ignored Joe and stared coolly at Buzz. "How did you know they've been here before?" she asked suspiciously.

"Because I've got one of the most expensive surveillance and security systems you've ever seen. Come on. I'll show you."

Nina and the Hardys climbed into Buzz McCord's truck and rode back to his ranch house. In his office, he showed them a wall of monitors just like the one Joe had seen at Wind Ridge Farm. Each monitor covered a different area of the farm. A video tape recorder was triggered every time someone entered or left one of the barns or came in through the main gate.

A young woman sat watching the screens and taking care of the VCR.

"You'll never see a camera, but I've got you covered coming and going," Buzz said with a friendly laugh. "Ginny, show them the tape of them arriving."

The brunette with the long silky ponytail pushed a couple of buttons on the console in front of her. One of the monitors went blank while the word *Rewinding* blinked on the screen. Then the picture came up again.

There was the small barn, and the time appeared on the screen. It said 7:50 A.M.

"Sorry, Mr. McCord," said Ginny, switching the machine into Fast Forward. "I went too far back."

"That's okay, Ginny," Buzz said.

Frank leaned toward the screen to watch. After a minute or two Ginny switched from Fast Forward back to Play, and everyone saw Frank, Joe, and Nina walking toward the barn. They saw Nina run to the fence and jump up. Then they saw Nina and Joe go into the barn while Frank stayed outside, looking at the tire tracks.

"I don't get it," Joe said. "Why are you showing us your whole security system?"

"To show you that I've got nothing to hide," Buzz said. "See, I'm getting a little tired of you boys being suspicious of me. And meanwhile you're not following up other leads. I don't want to think you're just jerking Nina's chain about this. A lot of folks around here care what happens to her."

"We care, too," Frank said. "Which is why I think we'd better take your advice and pursue some of those other leads. Come on, Joe. It's a long walk back to our car."

Joe looked at Frank questioningly, but the look Frank returned said, "Don't ask now. Wait—until we're alone."

Joe almost burst while he was waiting. Finally they were well away from McCord's ranch—and his video system and spying, prying recorders.

"Well? What? Tell me!" Joe said.

Frank smiled. "You saw the videotape of the barns, didn't you?"

"Yeah, so?" Joe said.

"After Ginny ran the tape back too far," Frank said, "I saw something very interesting. While she was scanning forward, I saw them load the black horse into a trailer and drive away."

"That's just what Buzz said happened," Nina said.

"Right. What's the big clue?" Joe said.

"Just this," Frank said. "The truck had writing on the door. In green letters it said Wind Ridge Farm. So if we want to find that horse, we know where to look!"

13 No Trespassing

"They took Nightmare to Wind Ridge?" Nina said excitedly. "Well, what are we waiting for? Let's go!"

But Joe aimed the car toward Stallion Canyon instead. "We'll check it out," he told Nina, "after we take you home."

"I don't want to go home!" Nina said, her eyes flashing. "I want to go with you to Wind Ridge and find Nightmare!"

"You can't," Joe explained as he drove south through the Sonoma hills. "Everyone knows you. And everyone knows that Nightmare was your horse. If we take you with us to Wind Ridge, they'll lock that place up tight, and Julian Ardyce will never come out of hiding!"

Nina didn't answer. She turned her head to the window and rode home in silence, her eyes slowly filling with tears.

"Good luck," she said softly when she hopped out of the car.

Joe drove to Wind Ridge Farm, whistling most of the way.

"I like a confident guy," Frank said. "You told Nina we'd know for sure where Nightmare is. That was a lot to promise."

"Big brother, we've got all the surprises on our side. Surprise number one: we say we know Ardyce really owns the farm, and we demand to see him. Of course we're bluffing, but if I'm right about those footprints I saw, the bluff just might work. Surprise number two: we tell Ardyce we know about the black horse that was being kept secretly on McCord's farm. Surprise number three: we reveal that we know the black horse was brought in this morning—by a Wind Ridge truck!"

Joe ignored the sign warning trespassers to keep out as he pulled into Wind Ridge Farm. "Yeah. We're going to slam the door on this case so hard San Francisco will think it's had another earthquake."

"Sounds good to me," Frank said.

Joe parked right in front of the stone and glass ranch house on the large complex and led the way into the house, past all the open rooms filled with

116

video monitors. Finally he stopped in front of Bill Barnell's office.

"This is it," Joe said to Frank.

"Hey, hold on there, son," called a voice. Taper was coming down the hall as fast as he could. "If you're thinking you can explain to Mr. Barnell why you disappeared and suddenly reappeared, you can save your breath. He doesn't want to see you."

Taper tried to move in front of Frank and Joe to block the doorway, but Joe moved faster and clamped his hand on the doorknob.

"We're not going to talk about my job," Joe said. "We want to talk to him about something else—a stolen horse."

Taper's smile closed, covering his shiny gold teeth. His voice grew serious. "Listen to me, son. You're going to cause yourself a whole lot of trouble with talk like that."

"I'm not your son," Joe said. "And our dad taught us how to start trouble *and* how to end it, too. Let's go, Frank."

Taper sighed and walked away. "I tried to warn you," he said over his shoulder.

Joe opened the door, and he and Frank stepped into the large, sunny office with its wall of monitors.

Bill Barnell sat behind his desk, watching the video screens. He stood up quickly and came around to the other side of his desk. Today he was wearing a jogging suit with his snakeskin cowboy boots. He looked around the room to see which monitors Frank and Joe were on. "What do you want?" asked Barnell. "You're fired."

"You can't fire me. I never really worked here," Joe said smugly. "I was just trying to get information—about Nightmare."

"What's that?" Barnell asked.

"Nightmare is a horse that was stolen about three years ago," Frank said. "We've been trying to find him, and we think he was brought here early this morning."

"There are no stolen horses on my ranch," Barnell said.

"Well, we'd like to hear that from the owner," Joe said. "From Julian Ardyce himself."

For a moment Barnell froze. His face didn't move, and he didn't say anything. He just stared at the monitors, almost as if he expected someone to appear on one of them and give him a good scolding.

"I'll be right back," Barnell said, stepping quickly out of the room.

"Well," Joe said with a grin, "I'd say surprise number one is working just fine."

"Yup," Frank said. He was letting his eyes roam across the papers and files on Barnell's desk.

"See anything interesting?" Joe asked, checking the door to be sure Barnell wasn't coming back.

"Not yet," Frank said. "There's probably better stuff in the desk drawers."

"Barnell could come back any second," Joe said.

"I'll bet you're faster than he is," Frank said with a smile.

"Yeah," said Joe, coming over to Barnell's desk and opening a drawer. There were notes, phone call messages, bills, and other papers in the top drawer. Then, in the second drawer, Joe found a notebook.

"Hey, Frank," Joe said, his voice rising with excitement. "This is it!"

"What?" Frank whispered the word.

"This notebook," Joe answered slowly. He was reading it as fast as he could. "It's got all the mating times for each mare on the farm. Here's Angel Eyes, two days ago, mated to Chain Letter."

Frank shrugged. "So?"

"Chain Letter is a stallion that stands here at Wind Ridge," Joe said. "I know because I mucked out his box the day I worked here."

"But you said they drove Angel Eyes to Buzz McCord's farm to be mated," Frank said.

Joe nodded. "They're lying, Frank. Why? Maybe it's because—"

Joe cut off his sentence. He saw Frank tap his ear with an index finger. Footsteps. Someone was coming.

Joe stuffed the notebook back in the drawer, and both brothers moved quickly back to their positions in the middle of the room. Then a private side door to the office—the door Barnell had used on his way out—opened slowly. Joe's heart raced in double time when a large man walked in. He was dressed in a black suit and a black silk shirt. It was Julian Ardyce! Even in his own house, he was carrying the black walking stick with the gold horse-head handle.

"You wanted to see me," Julian Ardyce said in a deep, throaty voice that filled the room.

Joe could hardly contain his excitement. He had been right! Ardyce did own the ranch, and now he and Frank were about to solve one of America's Most Mysterious Unsolved Crimes!

Ardyce moved to the desk and, with the tip of his cane, pushed a button. Instantly all of the monitors went black. Then he sat down behind the desk and looked at Joe as if he were a day-old sandwich in a cafeteria lunch line.

"Well, I must say that I am impressed," Ardyce said with a deep laugh. "A couple of boys have discovered where I live and that I am, indeed, the secret owner of Wind Ridge. And now that you have found out, what are you going to do? Run to the first newspaper you can find and sell your story? That's what I'd do, boys. There's money to be made off good old Julian Ardyce." He stood up like a dark cloud and waved his walking stick dramatically.

"That's not why we're here," Joe said. "We're looking for something."

"Oh?" Ardyce raised his eyebrows.

"Where is Nightmare?" Joe asked, springing surprise number two from its box.

Ardyce's face dropped. He leaned forward, resting both hands on his walking stick. "If there is justice is this world, that horse is a can of dog food right now," he said angrily. "Nightmare ruined my whole life."

Joe glanced at Frank with a puzzled look. Stealing a million-dollar horse had ruined his life?

"Boys, after that horse was stolen, no matter where I went, there were always people staring at me, TV reporters questioning me, accusing me—just as you two are doing now. I had to disappear from horse racing altogether, give up what I most dearly loved, because I couldn't endure seeing those faces every day."

The sound and the power of his voice were hypnotic, and Joe found himself feeling sympathetic toward and a little afraid of the man in black.

"There was a lot of evidence pointing in your direction," Frank said.

"But I am innocent," Ardyce said, slapping the end of his walking stick on the desk. "I had nothing to do with the theft of that horse. And no one has been able to prove that I did." Ardyce pointed his stick at Frank and then at Joe. "Tell me, now: can you prove that I stole that horse or are you here only to persecute me unjustly again?"

"No, we can't prove that you stole the horse," Joe said.

"Aha! Just as I thought," Ardyce said, shaking his

head at them. "Then you're just like all the rest—bolder and more cunning, perhaps, but you can't prove a thing."

Joe was getting hot—with both anger and embarrassment. He was beginning to wonder if Ardyce was right. Maybe they didn't have all the proof they needed. Maybe this was all a huge mistake. "What about the black horse Buzz McCord kept in a secret barn?"

"And what about it?" Ardyce said, as if he were teaching a class of first graders. "That horse is not mine. I own no black horses. As you might expect, I find them nothing but bad luck." He laughed again.

"That notebook in your desk says that Angel Eyes was mated to a horse that stands here," Joe said. "But I know Angel Eyes was taken over to Buzz McCord's farm."

"Young man, I thank you for bringing that fact to my attention," Ardyce said, bowing slightly to Joe. "If Mr. Taper has made a mistake, he will be fired immediately. I do not tolerate mistakes on my farm."

Time to try surprise number three, Joe thought. And Frank must have been thinking the same thing.

"We saw a Wind Ridge truck take that black horse from McCord's farm," Frank said.

"It's possible. I have a great many trucks," Ardyce said with a grand shrug. "I'm afraid I don't know where each one is every minute of the day. So,

122

you see, all you can do is accuse me of stealing. You cannot prove it."

"Give us half an hour to look around your farm and I'll bet we *can* prove it," Joe snapped. "I'll bet that black horse is here somewhere and you know it."

"Oh, no, boys. That's where you're wrong. I won't give you half an hour," Ardyce said, pushing another button on the desk with his stick. "I won't give you even another minute on my farm."

The door to the room opened quickly, and Taper and three other men walked in.

Ardyce glared down at Frank and Joe. "If you are seen sniffing around my farm again, you will be removed in as harsh and rude a manner as you can imagine." As he spoke, he walked around the desk and lightly touched Frank's and Joe's shirts, directly over their hearts, with the tip of his walking stick. "These gentlemen will see you to your car."

Taper and the three others pushed the Hardys out of the office and then outside to their car.

"I've started up the engine for you," Andy called from the driver's seat. "I knew you'd be in a hurry to leave."

Andy put the car in gear and hopped out. The car immediately started rolling away.

"Hey," Andy said, "what did I do? Forget to put on the brake?"

Frank and Joe took off after their runaway car, chasing it down the road.

Running as fast as he could, Joe almost caught the car. But it reached the crest of a small hill before he did. He could only watch as the car rolled down the hill. Then it picked up speed—and bounced off the road into a ditch!

14 At the Races

"Push!" Joe told himself as he tried to push and lift the front bumper of the car at the same time.

But the rental car was stuck stubbornly in the ditch. It took twenty minutes of grunting and sweating before Frank and Joe got the car back on the road.

"We'll be back," Joe called to a few of the ranch hands who had been watching them struggle with the automobile. But for the rest of the trip Joe and Frank rode in gloomy silence. There was no need to talk. Everything had gone wrong, and they both knew it. Joe had thought he had Ardyce nailed, but Ardyce had danced away. He thought they'd found Nightmare, but they hadn't come up with any proof. Joe knew his promise that they'd be back was a hollow threat.

As soon as the Hardys pulled into Stallion Canyon, Nina came out to meet them.

"Did you see him?" she asked excitedly. "Was it Nightmare? Was Ardyce there? Did you call the police?"

"We've got to talk," Joe said. But he knew his tone of voice had already told her most of the story.

Inside the house, Roger and Nina sat grimly listening to what happened.

"We saw Ardyce, and he even admitted that he owns Wind Ridge Farm. He's been hiding there since Nightmare was stolen," Frank said.

"But did you see any signs of Nightmare?" Roger asked.

"No," Frank said quietly. "Julian Ardyce wouldn't let us look around. We told him we saw one of his trucks take a black horse from Buzz McCord's farm, but Ardyce shrugged it off."

"He threw us off the farm," Joe said, still angry.

Nina picked up a magazine about thoroughbred racing and threw it across the room. "I'd like to throw *him* off the farm!" she yelled. "It's not fair!"

"So you don't really know that that horse was Nightmare, do you?" Mr. Glass asked.

Frank shook his head.

"But they've got to be hiding the black horse for a reason," Joe said. "And that horse is either at

Wind Ridge or back at McCord's ranch right now."

Mr. Glass sighed. "And until you find that horse, you aren't really any closer to knowing who stole Nightmare."

Frank shook his head again. He didn't look over at Nina, but he could hear her sniffling.

"Well, while you were gone, I talked to our lawyer," Mr. Glass said. "He said we'd never get a search warrant without more evidence, which we don't seem to have."

Frank and Joe were silent.

"Guys, I think we'd better close the subject," Mr. Glass said. "Nina and I can't think about this anymore. We've got a race to get ready for—starting right now, okay, Neen?"

Nina wiped her cheeks and sniffled once. "Okay, Dad," she said.

Close the subject? Frank thought to himself. Okay, if that's what they want. But we're not going to close the *case*. Not now—not when we've gotten this close.

"I understand your feelings," Frank said slowly. "But would you mind if we hung around for a few more days?"

"Yeah," Joe chimed in, shooting his brother a knowing glance. "Frank and I have gotten hooked on this thoroughbred business. I'd love to go with you to the track and see your horses race."

"Sure," Roger said. "Why not? Just promise me that you'll drop the detective stuff."

127

"No problem," Joe said. But he knew that he and Frank wouldn't give up until they'd solved the case.

The next day Joe and Frank helped Nina and her father load three horses into a large four-horse trailer. Then they drove to the track where the Santa Rosa Cup, a race for two-year-olds, was being held. The Glasses, like most other owners, were arriving a day early so the horses could get settled in before the race. One of the Glasses' horses, Imagine That, was among the top ten horses entered in the race.

As they walked through the stable area, watching other horses arrive in their trailers, Frank asked, "Will Buzz McCord and Wind Ridge Farm have entries in the race?"

"Give it a rest," Mr. Glass said. "You said you just wanted to stick around a couple of days to see the race."

"Right. Of course," Joe said emphatically.

Roger Glass shook his head. Then his mouth dropped open, and his eyes stared. "I don't believe it."

Frank turned to see what Roger was looking at. There, in the middle of the bustling stable area, was Julian Ardyce. He was making his way toward them through a small crowd of reporters, horse people, and stable hands.

"Hello, Glass," Ardyce said, waving his walking stick as he approached. "Hello, Nina. You certainly have grown to be a lovely young lady in these three years."

Frank watched Nina's reaction out of the corner of his eye. Her face grew tight and cold, and she gave Ardyce a killing glare.

"I'm surprised to see you, Julian," Roger Glass said, obviously feeling cool but not as angry as Nina.

"Well, these two young men are entirely responsible," Ardyce said, nodding at Frank and Joe. "Their visit convinced me that there was no reason for me to shy away from a public life any longer. And I'm not ashamed to say it: it feels mighty good to be back. How's your horse look, Glass?"

"He means, is he worth stealing, Dad," Nina said.

Anger, like a bolt of lightning, flashed across Ardyce's face. Then he leaned closer to Roger Glass. "She's still immature for her age, isn't she?" he said softly. "Well, good luck tomorrow."

Ardyce pointed his ebony stick, and the crowd of stable hands seemed to part so that the large dark cloud could move through.

"Nina," said her father, "could you run back to the truck? I think we left a bridle in back."

"In a minute, Dad," Nina said. "Look at that horse!"

Nina went running at top speed to one of the stalls farther down the line. Frank and Joe followed her to a sleek black horse.

"This horse," whispered Nina, "looks exactly

like Nightmare. Except for that clump of white at the base of the mane."

A groom, a young woman about twenty years old wearing baggy work clothes, came up from behind them and slipped into the stall. She stroked the horse's nose as she walked in.

"Whose horse is this?" Nina asked.

"This is River Run, miss," said the young woman in an Irish brogue. "She belongs to Mr. McCord. She's the favorite to win the cup, and she knows it. Look at the gleam in her eyes."

"Yeah," Nina said wistfully, as she petted the horse. "She looks like a champion."

When Nina was done petting the horse, Frank pulled her aside, out of earshot of the groom.

"Does that horse really look like Nightmare?" Frank asked.

"So much that it's spooky," Nina replied. "I mean, lots of fine thoroughbreds have similar characteristics—but not like that. That horse has Nightmare's build, coloring, stance, attitude, and something more. It's like she has the fire in her blood that Nightmare had."

"Maybe she does," Frank said.

"What do you mean?" Nina asked.

"Maybe that horse has Nightmare's blood in her. I mean, the way I figure it, River Run is two years old—just the right age to be Nightmare's offspring.

If McCord bred one of his mares with Nightmare the year he was stolen, the foal would be two years old today."

"You're right!" Nina shouted, and then clapped her hand over her mouth.

"So you think McCord stole Nightmare?" Joe whispered to his brother.

"Either Buzz took the horse or he's in on it with Julian Ardyce," Frank replied. "But we can't prove it."

Nina was looking back at River Run, staring at her with unblinking eyes as if she were trying to see deep into the horse's heart. "We could prove it with a blood test," she said finally.

"A blood test for horses?" Joe asked.

Nina nodded. "All racehorses are tattooed, and blood samples are taken to make sure the owner is telling the truth about the bloodlines on the horse's papers."

"You mean a blood test could prove that River Run is Nightmare's foal?" Joe said.

"Offspring," corrected Nina with a giggle. "Yes, just like with people."

"That puts McCord in a tough spot," Frank said. "He can't lie on the paperwork because the blood test will show the horse's real parents. What's left? Falsify the blood test? How does he think he'll get away with it?"

"I don't know what he's going to do," Nina said,

131

looking back at River Run. "But I wish I could have a blood test taken."

Frank's voice was low and even as he said, "Maybe you can—if we steal that horse. Just the way McCord stole Nightmare."

Nina's eyes flashed with excitement as she turned to meet Frank's gaze. She tossed her hair back, revealing a new pair of silver earrings—small stallions rearing up on their back legs. "Would you really do it?" she asked.

"Are you sure River Run looks *exactly* like Nightmare?" he replied.

"Yes," Nina said, her brows drawing together in a puzzled expression. "Except for the white hair on the mane. Nightmare is all black."

"Okay," Frank said. "Then tonight we prepare to steal River Run."

Joe whistled loudly. "Big brother, you are talking big trouble if we're wrong—or worse, if we get caught."

"I know," Frank said. "It's not just dangerous, it's stupid. Besides, we don't really have to steal the horse to get a blood sample, but it's the only way I can think of to make McCord confess. I'm hoping we can duplicate his crime exactly, and he'll realize he's been caught. If you think this is too crazy, Joe, say so now."

"It's too crazy," Joe said. Then he smiled. "But count me in."

"What do we do?" Nina asked.

"First, we need to find another black horse we can substitute. A horse we can disguise to look like River Run," Frank said.

Nina smiled, and her green eyes glowed. "How about our horse Party Girl? We brought Party Girl from Stallion Canyon, and she runs in the first race tomorrow. If I paint a patch of her mane after she runs, she'll look just like River Run."

"That'll be your job tomorrow, then," Frank said.

"What are you going to do?" Nina asked.

"Joe and I are going to try to sneak into the racing office tonight and make up a fake release form. We'll use it to get River Run out of the racetrack, using Party Girl's release papers. And your dad will still have Party Girl's real papers."

"Nina, can you get your vet to meet us?" Joe said. "It won't take McCord long to notice the switch and we'll need the proof fast."

"What if we're wrong?" Nina asked, suddenly looking worried.

"Come visit us in jail," Frank said nervously.

Late that night, Frank and Joe walked casually through the parking lot of the racetrack, acting as if they had every right in the world to be there. They made their way to the racing office. The small cinder-block building that had no air conditioning was closed for the night and dark, but Joe quickly discovered a window that wasn't locked.

"Let me know if someone's coming," Frank said, as Joe boosted him in through the window.

In the dark, with only his pocket flashlight, Frank hunted through the office until he found some blank release forms. He typed in Party Girl as the horse's name. Then he came to a space for the tattoo. What *is* River Run's tattoo number? Frank wondered. Well, it was too late—and too dangerous—to find out now. Frank made up a number and forged the signatures on the form.

I hope Nina can talk the guard out of checking River Run's tattoo tomorrow, he thought, because it won't match the one on the form.

Finally the release form was done, and Frank tucked it inside his shirt. All he had to do then was get out of there—fast.

Frank poked his head out of the open window and looked into the darkness. "Joe," he called in his loudest whisper. "I'm coming down."

"Okay," Joe whispered back.

Frank swung one leg out the window and then the other. Then he turned around, held on to the windowsill, and began to lower himself to the ground.

Partway down, Frank felt hands grab his legs, trying to pull him down fast.

"Stop joking around," Frank told his brother.

But the hands held on even tighter, jerking him to

the ground. He landed on the dirt with a thud. When a voice broke the silence, it gave Frank a chill.

"You've got a lot of explaining to do," said a man.

Frank's heart began doing aerobics. It wasn't Joe standing over him. It was Julian Ardyce!

15 Horse Thieves

"I wanted to warn you," Joe said, stepping out from behind Julian Ardyce.

"But I told him I'd pull you down and break your legs if he did," Julian Ardyce interrupted, adding a small laugh. "That's the wonderful thing about threats. They're so effective because they might be true. One never knows."

"Don't sweat it, Joe," Frank said, waiting to see what Ardyce's next move was going to be.

"Sneaking out of the track office window at midnight," Ardyce said, shaking his head at Frank. "Now, what kind of plausible explanation can you boys have for that?"

Frank glared at the large man who was playing a

teasing game of cat and mouse. Frank didn't like being the mouse one bit.

"I want to know what you're up to," Ardyce repeated.

Frank let out a deep breath, trying to sound cool and calm when he spoke. "I thought I saw a light and some moving shadows in the office. So I climbed up to investigate."

"And what did you find?" Ardyce asked. He poked Frank's chest with his walking stick, right where Frank had hidden the race track release form. Frank hoped with all his might that Ardyce couldn't feel it.

"Nothing," Frank said.

"So you just happened to be walking around near the office at midnight?" Julian Ardyce said.

"Sure. Just like you," Joe said, trying to sound as challenging as Ardyce.

Ardyce was silent for a moment. Frank could see the man calculating all the possibilities and all the risks.

"You know," Ardyce said, brushing track dust off his oversize black jacket, "I don't think we have any more to say to one another." With that, he turned and walked away.

"We'll see about that tomorrow," Joe said softly when the big man was out of sight.

By three o'clock the next afternoon, Joe's nerves

were beginning to fray. The hustle and bustle in the stables provided a perfect cover for the activities that he and Frank had planned. But the waiting was killing him.

The narrow avenue between the two long wooden barns was crowded with horses going to and coming from their races. All kinds of people clogged the path, too—owners, trainers, photographers, jockeys in their colorful racing silks. But Nina still hadn't shown up. She was sitting in the spectators' box with her father, Joe knew, waiting for the right moment to slip away and carry out her part of the plan.

Frank and Joe wandered through the crowds, dodging horses and people.

Finally, near River Run's box, they heard a voice.

"Frank! Joe!" Nina called anxiously.

Joe spun around and saw Nina.

"I'm ready," she whispered. "I've got Party Girl waiting in a stall nearby."

"Great. Let's get this show on the road," Joe said. He moved closer to River Run's box.

Lucky break for our team, Joe thought. The only person with the horse was the young woman with the Irish brogue. She was brushing and patting the horse.

"Hi," Joe said coolly. "Mr. McCord's asking for you."

"Surely you don't mean now?" said the woman, giving Joe a strange look.

138

Joe gave her his most innocent face. "He said immediately. That's all I know."

The woman shrugged. "Men," she said, shaking her head as she walked past Joe and closed the door to the box behind her.

Joe watched her leave and looked around to make certain no one was paying attention. He opened the door to the box while his eyes continued to scan the area. He had only a few minutes. The woman would soon find McCord and realize that he didn't want to see her. Joe grabbed the horse's reins and tried to back her out of her box. But the horse pulled back and refused to move.

"Come on," Joe coaxed, pulling on the reins again. "Come on, girl." This time the horse followed him out of the box.

Joe saw Nina and Frank coming quickly in the opposite direction, leading Party Girl. They looked at one another as they passed. Nina was pale and tense. Frank's eyes were like searchlights, watching the crowd for McCord.

Joe walked on, slowly leading River Run away. He found himself counting the seconds in his head. Two minutes had gone by. Would Frank and Nina put Party Girl in the box and get out of there before McCord caught them?

Suddenly Joe felt a tap on his shoulder. He jerked involuntarily.

"We put Party Girl to bed," Frank said quietly, moving ahead to clear a path in the crowd.

139

"The trailer's waiting," Nina told Joe.

They walked River Run away from the crowd, to a deserted area behind the barns where they loaded the horse into a Stallion Canyon trailer. Then with a relieved sigh, Joe started to drive the car to the exit gate.

"We're almost home," Frank said.

"I'm scared. I can't breathe," Nina said.

"Don't breathe. But be sure to smile at the guards when we get to the gate," said Joe. "If they check the tattoo, we're dead."

Joe slowed down next to a small aluminum guard-house. The hood of the car was almost touching the wooden rail fence that blocked the road in front.

Two guards were sitting inside, listening to the radio. "Whatcha got there?" asked one. He stepped out of the guardhouse and walked up to the car.

"Sick horse," Joe said.

"Too bad," said the guard.

Frank passed the guard the release papers from the backseat. "Yeah, she went lame."

"Thanks," said the guard. "I just need to check the mouth — well, never mind. Better get her to the vet pronto."

Joe saluted the guard and hit the gas pedal.

After a breath, Frank said from the backseat, "We're clear. Congratulations. We're now official horse thieves."

"Now I *really* can't breathe," Nina said, shivering suddenly.

"Where to?" Joe asked.

"Drive one mile down the road and pull off into the empty field," Nina said. "You can leave us there. I'll watch River Run until our vet comes. He promised to take the blood sample for me, but he says if we're wrong he's going to lock me away himself."

Frank and Joe left Nina and ran all the way back to the racetrack.

"I hope we get to see McCord's face when he realizes what happened," Joe said.

"I'll be satisfied with hearing his confession," Frank said.

They returned to the stable area to find the narrow path still crowded with people and horses. But Frank and Joe also saw TV and radio news crews pushing and shoving around River Run's box.

Joe pushed through first. He squeezed into the middle of the crowd until he and Frank were close enough to hear and almost close enough to see everything that was happening.

"Of course I'm sure this isn't my horse!" Buzz McCord was bellowing. His face was as red as the shirt he was wearing. For once he wasn't wearing his mirrored sunglasses, and his eyes looked wild. "Just look at her lip. That's not River Run's number. Someone stole my horse and swapped it for this nag. They're checking in the office, and as soon as they tell me whose horse this is I'm going to string him up myself!"

141

Suddenly one of the TV camera crews recognized Julian Ardyce, who was standing to one side of the crowd. They swung their cameras, microphones, and lights in his direction.

"Mr. Ardyce, how do you feel about the fact that your horse won the Santa Rosa Cup today when Mr. McCord's horse was unable to race?" a reporter asked.

"No comment," Ardyce said, nervously fingering the golden horse-head handle of his walking stick. But the reporters' questions kept coming.

"Mr. Ardyce, isn't this exactly what happened three years ago when your horse won the California Classic after Nightmare was stolen?"

Frank and Joe could see that Ardyce was sweating noticeably.

"No comment," he said again.

"Mr. Ardyce, don't you think it's a strange coincidence that the day you make your first public appearance in three years, another horse is stolen?"

"Are you accusing and convicting me already, you obnoxious vultures?" Ardyce shouted, waving his walking stick angrily to clear an escape path for himself. He left with a trail of reporters following him.

"McCord isn't going to crack," Frank told Joe. "He's a cool one."

"Yeah," Joe said. "But meanwhile the media are ready to lynch Julian Ardyce."

"I'd like to see the tree that could hold him," Frank joked. "Come on. We'd better talk to Ardyce."

Frank and Joe pushed their way through the barn until they caught up with Ardyce, who was walking away from the track.

"Mr. Ardyce! Mr. Ardyce," Frank shouted, finally cutting in front of him.

"It's starting again. Flap-flap-flap—the vultures picking at the flesh." Ardyce spat the words. His face was pale and lined with a sadness that seemed to come from deep in his heart. "It's not fair. I am no more guilty of stealing that horse than I am of stealing Nightmare."

"I know," Frank said.

Ardyce stared at him with suspicion.

"Mr. Ardyce, we know exactly who stole River Run," Joe said.

"And who might that be?"

"We did," Frank said.

Ardyce's eyes enlarged to twice their size.

"Right now," Frank explained, "River Run is having a blood test to see if she is the offspring of Nightmare."

"And you think she is?" Ardyce said.

Joe shrugged. "I don't know, but Nina Glass thinks so. And once we know for sure, it won't take us very long to piece everything together."

"I believe that you didn't steal Nightmare,"

Frank said, "but I think you know a lot about what happened to him. Why don't you tell the truth? It's still not too late to help Nina get her horse back."

Ardyce sighed a long, deep sigh. Then he turned and walked back to the stable where the TV reporters were interviewing Buzz McCord. Frank and Joe followed.

"Ladies and gentlemen," Ardyce announced. "If I may have your attention, please."

The crowd quieted almost at the first sound of his voice.

"Thank you," said Julian Ardyce. As he looked around at the crowd he seemed nervous and, for once, speechless. "I would like to tell you who really stole Nina Glass's horse, Nightmare."

16 The Truth Revealed

Frank felt the reporters and horse people moving in around Julian Ardyce, pushing him closer to the enormous man.

Was Ardyce really going to tell the whole world who stole Nightmare? Frank held his breath, and for a moment his eyes and Ardyce's locked. In Ardyce's stare, Frank saw pain and regret, but also a little admiration. Then Ardyce looked away, stared into the spotlights of the video cameras, and began to speak.

"I know that for most of you this will come as a shock," he said, smiling jovially. "But I did not steal Nightmare of Stallion Canyon three years ago. I know how disappointed you are to think that the man you have insulted and hounded for so long is innocent."

"Then who stole the horse?" called a reporter.

"You don't know, do you? None of you know." Ardyce was mocking them. "It took two young detectives only a week to discover the truth. The truth is that Buzz McCord stole Nightmare and has kept the horse in a hidden stable on his farm ever since."

Everyone in the crowd started murmuring and talking at once.

"That's a complete lie!" Buzz McCord shouted. He was standing in one of the stalls where his horses were kept.

Ardyce shook his head and pointed his walking stick at McCord. "I know it's the truth because for the last three years I have paid this man enormous fees to breed my mares with Nightmare. That horse has made him rich."

Roger Glass had been standing off to the side, but now he pushed his way through the crowd. "Julian, where is Nightmare now?" he demanded.

"Nightmare is on my farm, right where these two"—Ardyce gestured toward the Hardys— "suspected he was. He was transported there yesterday morning when McCord thought they were going to discover him."

I knew it! Frank thought. Immediately, the questions started coming from every direction as reporters shouted to Ardyce and all the onlookers talked at once.

"How did he steal Nightmare?" "Who stole River Run?" "What does he mean about two detectives?"

Frank felt a tap on his shoulder. Two police officers had arrived—detectives. They were circulating through the crowd, picking out the key players.

"Come with me," one of the officers said.

Frank, Joe, Ardyce, Roger Glass, and Buzz McCord were all rounded up and taken to the second-floor racing office in the concrete-block building.

Inside, Frank and Joe and Roger Glass sat on old wooden desks pushed up against the walls while Buzz McCord and Ardyce sat in chairs in the middle of the floor. The police detectives stood with their arms crossed, trying to get the story straight.

"Now, what happened today? Could someone start at the beginning?" said the officer who had identified himself as Lieutenant Markle.

"Somebody stole my horse. That's all I have to say," McCord barked stubbornly.

"My brother and I stole River Run," Frank admitted, staring straight at McCord. "We did it exactly the way you stole Nightmare. Before the race we

147

substituted a horse that looked like River Run. It was easy. With all the activity, no one paid any attention to a couple of people leading horses around. We even used forged release papers to take River Run away from the track—just as you must have."

McCord's face didn't move.

"And right now," Joe said, "River Run is having her blood tested, which will help us prove who her real father is. We think it's Nightmare. What do you think, Mr. McCord?"

McCord's face folded, and his hands dropped into his lap. "I guess it's over," he mumbled. "Well, okay."

"Okay, what?" asked Lieutenant Markle, who was taking notes.

"Okay, it's true. I admit it. I stole Nightmare."

Frank looked over at Joe, who gave him a thumbs-up sign.

"How'd you do it?" Lieutenant Markle asked as he scraped a wooden chair along the floor and sat down right in front of McCord. "You can hear me, can't you, McCord?"

McCord cleared his throat about every two words. "It's just like they said. I hired a guy I could trust to take Nightmare out and substitute one of Ardyce's horses in his stall. I used phony release papers, the whole works. Even the groom was no problem. I just paid Danny Chaps a thousand bucks to go get a can of soda for half an hour."

148

"Who else helped you, Mr. McCord?" asked Lieutenant Markle, leaning closer.

McCord wiped moisture from his upper lip. "Will it go easier for me if I tell you?"

"It'll just go harder if you don't," answered the police officer.

"Al Provo," McCord said quietly. He cleared his throat again and said it louder.

Lieutenant Markle turned to one of his officers. "Get Provo in here," he said.

The officer left the small office quickly.

"Lieutenant Markle," Frank said, "I have a couple of questions."

The policeman stood up, nodding at Frank.

"You've been trying to scare us off the case from the first day, haven't you, McCord?" Frank said. "You tried pushing us in front of a cable car, launching us in a hot air balloon, knocking us out, and leaving us at Alcatraz."

Lieutenant Markle laughed. "You guys have had a busy week," he said.

"I don't know what you're talking about," McCord said.

Frank clenched his teeth. That was a lie, and McCord knew it. But before he could say anything else, the door opened. The police officer walked in with a tall, muscular man. Behind them trailed a young blond guy. It was the stable hand who had whispered to Frank at McCord's ranch just before his horse took off.

149

"Al Provo?" asked Lieutenant Markle.

The tall man nodded.

"You've just been named as an accomplice in the theft of Nightmare," Lieutenant Markle said.

Provo glared at McCord. "Thanks, pal," he snarled.

"Look at the other guy," Joe whispered to Frank. "Look at his jacket."

Frank looked at the blond guy. He was wearing a denim jacket with one torn sleeve.

"Lieutenant Markle," Frank said quickly, pointing to the blond kid, "that's the guy who pushed us in front of the cable car! We've got a witness."

The blond guy looked at Frank and then at McCord. He had the eyes of a trapped animal.

"You don't have to say anything, Lonnie," McCord warned him.

"I knew I was going to get into trouble, but it wasn't my idea. None of that stuff was," Lonnie said, ignoring McCord. "Mr. McCord said he had a couple guys he wanted us to 'discourage.'"

"Us?" Lieutenant Markle asked quickly.

"Provo and me," Lonnie said.

"Thanks," Al Provo snarled again. "I got lots of pals in this room."

"You and Provo dragged us to Alcatraz?" Joe asked.

"Yeah," Lonnie said. "We did all of that stuff. Mr. McCord said he'd fire me if I didn't, and I really need this job."

McCord suddenly laughed. "When Lonnie slipped a burr under Blackbeard's saddle blanket, I thought you'd take a ride you'd always remember," he said, looking at Frank and his brother with a mixture of anger and amusement. "All I can say is, you two must be tougher than cowhide."

Nobody seemed to have anything else to add, so Lieutenant Markle stopped writing in his notebook. "Well, I guess that's all we need to know for now."

"No, it's not," said a voice at the back of the small, hot room. Nina stepped forward. Her cheeks were wet, and her voice shook with anger. "Why, Buzz? I want to know why you did this. How could you pretend to be our friend when you had Nightmare all the time?"

McCord shifted uncomfortably on his chair, crossing and uncrossing his legs. "I don't expect you to understand this, Nina, but sometimes a fellow gets tired of working for the guys who have all the money. Sometimes that fellow wants some of the money for himself. I'm sorry about hurting you."

"I guess I can understand that, Buzz," Nina said in a cold voice, "but I can't forgive you." Then she ran out of the room.

McCord tightened his bottom lip and nodded a couple times. "Well, what now?" he asked.

"You're under arrest, Mr. McCord," said Markle. With a nod of his head, he motioned toward the door. "Let's go to the station."

151

Frank and Joe went outside to find Nina and Roger Glass. Nina was standing with her back to the office, not watching the police taking McCord away.

"Dad," Nina said, "I want to see Nightmare. Right away."

Roger Glass nodded and called to Julian Ardyce. "We're on our way over to your place to pick up Nightmare."

"Of course. Come ahead," Ardyce said. "I'll meet you there."

When the Glasses and the Hardys finally drove into Wind Ridge Farm, they found Julian Ardyce standing in an open field. With him was a tall, strong, beautiful black horse with no saddle and no bridle.

Nina inhaled sharply the moment she saw him. "I can't believe it," she said. "It's Nightmare! It's really him!"

She jumped out of the car, ran a few steps, then slowed to a walk. She climbed the fence and lowered herself lightly to the ground. Then she turned and started walking to the horse as Julian Ardyce walked away.

Frank, Joe, and Roger came up and leaned on the fence, watching without saying a word.

Nightmare raised his head, sniffing the air and shaking his head from side to side. Then he began to move toward Nina.

The girl stood motionless as the horse circled her

152

and came close. Then Nightmare lowered his head and nudged Nina, making her take two steps back. Then he did it again.

"He remembers me!" Nina shouted, laughing with tears rolling down her cheeks.

In the open field, Nina climbed up on Nightmare's back, and the horse trotted off with the girl hugging her horse around its neck.

"I want to thank you," Mr. Glass said, turning to Frank and Joe. "Somehow I've got to find a way to thank you."

"How about this?" said Julian Ardyce, handing Frank his ebony walking stick with the gold horsehead handle. "If you don't mind, Glass."

Mr. Glass shook his head.

"Important people carry a walking stick, boys, and I can't count on being important after today. You proved me innocent of one crime that's haunted me, boys. But I confessed to another— being an accessory, albeit after the fact. I wonder if they'll prosecute me." Ardyce tapped the horse's head with one of his large fingers. "It's real gold, you know. It has to be real gold, boys."

"Thanks, Mr. Ardyce," said Frank, admiring the walking stick as he turned it in his hands.

Joe cleared his throat. "Let me see that," he said. "The gold horse head matches my hair."

"You mean it matches your head for *hardness!*" Frank said with a laugh, handing the walking stick to Joe.

They watched Nina and Nightmare gallop away and disappear into the golden sunlit distance.

"You know, I've been waiting for years for this, and it's finally happened," said Joe.

"You've been waiting for a walking stick?" Frank asked with surprise.

"No. For a client to ride off into the sunset! Now, that's what I call a happy ending!"